Providence:
Hannah's Journey

Barbara M. Britton

*Blessings on
your journey*

Barbara M Britton

Hannah & Gilead II Kings 5

D0596782

This is a work of fiction. Names, characters, places, and incidents either are the product of the author's imagination or are used fictitiously, and any resemblance to actual persons living or dead, business establishments, events, or locales, is entirely coincidental.

Providence

COPYRIGHT 2015 by Barbara M. Britton

All rights reserved. No part of this book may be used or reproduced in any manner whatsoever without written permission of the author or Pelican Ventures, LLC except in the case of brief quotations embodied in critical articles or reviews.

eBook editions are licensed for your personal enjoyment only. eBooks may not be re-sold, copied or given away to other people. If you would like to share an eBook edition, please purchase an additional copy for each person you share it with.

Contact Information: titleadmin@pelicanbookgroup.com

All scripture quotations, unless otherwise indicated, are taken from the Holy Bible, New International Version(R), NIV(R), Copyright 1973, 1978, 1984, 2011 by Biblica, Inc.™ Used by permission of Zondervan. All rights reserved worldwide. www.zondervan.com

Cover Art by *Nicola Martinez*

Harbourlight Books, a division of Pelican Ventures, LLC
www.pelicanbookgroup.com PO Box 1738 *Aztec, NM * 87410

Harbourlight Books sail and mast logo is a trademark of Pelican Ventures, LLC

Publishing History
First Harbourlight Edition, 2016
Paperback Edition ISBN 978-1-61116-844-0
Electronic Edition ISBN 978-1-61116-842-6
Published in the United States of America

Dedication

To my family who inspires me each and every day.

Acknowledgements

This book would not have been possible without the help of so many people. My first and foremost thank you goes to my family. They have been my cheering section throughout my publishing journey and they never doubted that someday one of my books would be in print.

To everyone at Pelican Book Group who took a chance on a debut author writing Biblical Romantic Adventures. Thank you Nicola Martinez and Sarah Grimm for championing Hannah's story.

I have a marvelous critique partner, Betsy Norman, who pushes me to make my writing better and who has a big crush on Gilead. And to the Barnes & Noble Brainstormers who keep my word counts up and share hot chocolate with me, thank you Jill Bevers, Liz Czukas, Karen Miller, Betsy Norman, Liz Steiner, and Sandee Turriff. I have a huge support system within the WisRWA community and too many friends who have encouraged me weekly or monthly to name. I am grateful.

To my Pitch Wars mentor Molly Lee who happened to be looking for Bible-themed YA. She gave her time and talent to help me make this story better. And to Brenda Drake who makes Pitch Wars possible. The Pitch Wars name sounds menacing but it is an awesome mentoring program for unpublished writers.

My church family has encouraged me through all the ups and downs of publishing. I am blessed to have their support.

And last, but definitely not least, to the Lord God Almighty, for giving me the gift of creativity and breath each day to write these stories.

Acknowledgements

This book would not have been possible without the help of so many people. My first and foremost thank you goes to my family. They have been my cheering section throughout my publishing journey and they never doubted that someday one of my books would be in print.

To everyone at Pelican Book Group who took a chance on a debut author writing Biblical Romantic Adventures. Thank you Nicola Martinez and Sarah Grimm for championing Hannah's story.

I have a marvelous critique partner, Betsy Norman, who pushes me to make my writing better and who has a big crush on Gilead. And to the Barnes & Noble Brainstormers who keep my word counts up and share hot chocolate with me, thank you Jill Bevers, Liz Czukas, Karen Miller, Betsy Norman, Liz Steiner, and Sandee Turriff. I have a huge support system within the WisRWA community and too many friends who have encouraged me weekly or monthly to name. I am grateful.

To my Pitch Wars mentor Molly Lee who happened to be looking for Bible-themed YA. She gave her time and talent to help me make this story better. And to Brenda Drake who makes Pitch Wars possible. The Pitch Wars name sounds menacing but it is an awesome mentoring program for unpublished writers.

My church family has encouraged me through all the ups and downs of publishing. I am blessed to have their support.

And last, but definitely not least, to the Lord God Almighty, for giving me the gift of creativity and breath each day to write these stories.

1

Hannah waited mere feet from the prophet of Israel, shaded from the Jerusalem sun by the sprawling branches of a tamarisk tree. Sweat beaded beneath her head covering, a result of the mid-summer heat, her nerves, or both. A crowd hung back, blocking the Horse Gate and lining the city's massive stone walls. They had come to see the man of God heal the lame and the cursed.

Hannah bore a curse since birth. For seventeen years, she had been unable to taste or smell. Her ears were but a flap of skin with no slope, no lobe. Her father said it was a punishment from God for an ancestor's crime. As the chief priest, he should know.

She grasped her father's velvet robe as the prophet's hands slid over a young boy's leg. The boy had lain in his father's arms not two feet from Hannah and her father and brother, his limb nothing but a boiled bone with skin. She shook with anticipation as she witnessed sun-toasted flesh, fat as a baby's cheek, grow on top of the boy's decomposed leg. *What will it feel like when the prophet touches my nose, my lips, my ears?*

"Will it hurt?" she asked, looking to her father.

Shimron, her brother, bent low. "Not as much as our humiliation. Will not everyone hear that the chief

1

priest's daughter is in need of healing?" Shimron scanned the mass of people. "To think the prophet refused us a private ceremony."

"Hush," her father warned, glancing to see if the holy one listened.

She fought to keep her composure. *I am a disgrace.*

Shrieks of "*Jehovah Jireh*" sliced the arid breeze.

"God has healed me," the boy shouted. He jumped on his re-birthed leg, arms flapping as if to fly away and leave the hardened ground behind.

Hannah stifled a gleeful laugh. She delighted in the boy's ecstatic dance.

The man of God turned toward her. He reached out the same hand that had healed the boy and pointed at her chest. "Come."

She stiffened. Her heart fluttered faster than a startled sparrow. As she shuffled forward, Shimron took hold of her tunic and yanked her nearer to the prophet. "It has been seventeen years," he whispered. "Do not make him wait for the likes of you."

Trembling, she dropped to her knees before the prophet and beheld his weathered face.

His hands rested on her shoulders with a firm, yet gentle press. "What is your given name?"

"Hannah," she whispered, struggling to speak, her tongue dry as linen. "Daughter of Zebula, a Levite—"

"I know of your lineage." The prophet grinned and looked to her father and brother. "Not of your condition."

Hannah hesitated. Her father had forbidden her to speak of the curse. Her hair and head covering had hidden her deformed ears. She glanced up for her father's permission. He gave her a reassuring nod.

Lifting her veil, she revealed the nub of an ear.

"My tongue does not taste food," she began, meeting the holy man's gaze. "My nose breathes, but I cannot smell the world around—"

"She has burned her hem to ashes many times in the cooking fires," Shimron cut in. "She does not eat. Wheat chaff weighs more than my sister."

Her back straightened, but she continued to concentrate on the prophet's aged face.

The man of God ignored Shimron and cupped her jaw. His thumbs caressed her cheekbones, her ears, and stroked to the bridge of her nose.

Hannah closed her eyes. Her body went weightless under the prophet's touch, almost free from her burden. She dreamed of things the warm breeze would blow her way—a woman's perfume, the stench of the unwashed. Things she had only heard of before. But nothing came.

The prophet's fingers stilled. He drew back from her.

Surely she should feel something? A burning on her tongue? A tingling in her nose? A tickling in her ears? She prayed for pain.

"It is not her time," the man of God said, his voice steady, yet quiet.

Stunned, she sat back, bracing herself so she would not collapse further into the dirt.

"But she has been without her senses since birth. And that skin." Her father tried to display the side of her face as he pulled her to her feet and pushed her closer to the prophet. "Surely it is not of her doing. What sin could a child commit to cause this punishment?"

Hannah drew to her full height at her father's declaration of innocence. The attention of the people centered on her and on her family. Sweat trickled down her arm.

"Please," Hannah said as the holy one started to leave. "I have asked forgiveness."

Shimron grabbed the prophet's arm. "Heal her," he demanded. "My family has sacrificed for her sins."

"And so you should," the prophet answered. He glanced at Hannah.

She clutched her brother's hand and withdrew it from the man of God.

"You healed the boy," she said with rushed breaths. The prophet's anointed-one stare twisted her stomach into a weaver's knot.

"The power and timing do not belong to me." The righteous man turned from her. His regal gait parted the crowd. Trailed by a servant, he headed away from Jerusalem.

The muttering of the crowd grew louder. Hannah's cheeks warmed as if she were bending over a cooking fire. She noticed all the curious people studying her. *They know something's wrong with me.* How could her mother deny the gossip with all these witnesses? Hannah turned to find her father and brother discussing her, their faces close, their words terse.

The crowd shifted forward to hear the conversation between the angry, insulted priests. Their glances condemned her. Their judgments slandered her mother. Her composure crumbled. She lifted the hem of her tunic and raced toward the city gate.

"Do not touch her," a man yelled. "She is unclean."

"Leave me be," Hannah cried. She pushed a woman out of the way and fled down the nearest street.

Her sandals thudded against the dirt lane as she dodged oxen and carts and merchants. Her chest burned as if the dust particles she breathed were embers from a blacksmith's fire. Her father should not have taken her to the prophet. He should have accepted her fate. She was cursed. A vessel of sin birthed from the past.

She looked over her shoulder to see if anyone pursued her. *Selah!* No one did.

Linens hung by the side of the road, drying in the heat. She slipped behind a cotton shield strung between two buildings, creating a small alcove. She hid by a fat rain barrel and tried to calm her breathing, but the pressure behind her eyes caused her chest to cave even deeper. Supported by the wall of a stranger's home, she buried her face in her knees. What would her mother say to the holy man's refusal?

Footsteps crunched against the ground, coming closer to the linen wall. Was it her father? She wrapped her arms around her knees and pulled her legs tight to her body. The curtain whipped back. Sunlight blinded her. Blinking, she focused on a young man, his turban barely able to contain his wild, curly black hair. His eyes widened and he rubbed his bearded jaw line, giving himself an imaginary shave with his finger.

Hannah leaned backward into the clay bricks of the wall. "Don't touch me," she warned. Her throat tightened from the run and the erratic beat of her heart.

He squatted down in front of her. His height and muscular body dwarfed her tiny hide-out. "Why? Are you sick? Hurt?"

"No." She shifted further from the man, not wanting to explain about the prophet. "Can't you leave me be?"

"A young woman sits where I lie—"

Hannah shot to her feet. "This is not a bed." Her gaze darted around the alcove. Her heart wrestled with her ribs. "You do not expect me to believe you sleep here?"

"Mostly here." The man rose slowly and pointed to an area between the barrel and some crates stacked in the corner.

"Not inside?" She glanced up the stone wall to a window above them.

"Only when my fath...my mother's husband is away."

Hannah's spine flattened against the wall. She surveyed the dark-haired intruder's face in case she would need to recall him later. He looked not much older than she. Dark brown mischievous eyes stared back at her, sparkling as if he had captured the glow of the moon he slept under. Did he think she had money to steal? Or worse, would he take her virginity? She glanced at the sheet billowing in the breeze, hiding them from sight. Could she race fast enough back to the street? She slid a ruby bracelet under her sleeve. It was to have been a gift for the prophet when he had healed her. There was no need to tempt this man with gold and gems.

"Are you hungry?"

"What?" The hospitable offer of food shattered her thoughts of escape.

He rummaged inside a sack tied to his belt and offered a pomegranate. "Sit and share with me. Looks like you could use some." He carefully removed a carving knife from the woven bag and sliced off a piece of the honeycombed fruit, revealing bright red berries.

2

Hannah wilted from the heat of the cooking fire, but she would rather be in the secluded courtyard at home, than facing mockery from citizens on the streets. She skimmed burnt paste off the top of her stewed figs and tried to salvage some of the fruit. As the sole daughter of Zebula, the chore of preparing supper lay at her feet. *Oh, why couldn't the prophet have healed my nose?* She handed a spoon to the wife of her brother Shimron. "Can you taste the ash?"

Her sister-in-law, Rebekah, wrinkled her nose. "If you do not tell, perhaps they will think it a new spice."

Hannah groaned. She had already made one trip to the well in the heat of the day. Now she needed more water to start over. At least the afternoon sun kept the whisperers away. Three Sabbaths had passed since the prophet's refusal to heal her. Three Sabbaths and the prophet had not returned to Jerusalem. Three Sabbaths and the people remembered her shame, even if they did not know its origin.

Pulling her head covering low to hide her face, she walked several streets until she reached the well. As she neared its round, stone wall, a woman hurried off, sloshing precious water from her jar. Had she too, been at the gate that day? Hannah carefully wrapped her hand in white cloth before hoisting the bucket. She filled her jar, lifted it onto her shoulder, and used it as a shield from the curious eyes of the street dwellers.

When Hannah returned home, her aunt sat in a shaded corner of the cooking courtyard, rubbing Rebekah's rounded belly.

Hannah greeted her aunt with a kiss on the cheek.

"I will come to help birth Rebekah's baby," her aunt said.

Hannah poured water into a fresh pot and began serving the remainder to her aunt and sister-in-law. "I will also care for the babe."

Her aunt took a generous sip. "What about Azor's children? Will you not care for them in Hebron?"

Hannah's pulse quickened. Her stomach plummeted into an imaginary well, coming up empty. She looked to Rebekah for a glimpse of understanding. Hannah's fingers trembled as she held a cup of drink out to her sister-in-law. "Why would I mother Azor's children? I am not his wife."

"You will be." Her aunt spoke in pronouncement of a well-known truth.

Hannah clutched her waist. Surely, her father had not arranged a secret betrothal. To Azor no less. A priest twice her age with children as old as she. "Father has praised Azor's service. He is a respected priest, but no word has come to me of his interest in another wife." She held her voice steady, willing her words to be true.

Her aunt's eyes narrowed. "Your father has not spoken of the widower?"

Hannah shook her head. Her stomach churned at the thought of being bound to an old, shriveled stranger. What did Azor have to offer her? Nursemaid? Servant? Hannah's breaths caught in her chest. "My father and brother have been receiving offerings at the temple. There has been no mention of my—"

"Soon," her aunt stated in the definite tone of an elder. "You will do what is chosen."

Hannah shivered as if a locust had crawled down her back. She turned away from her aunt and Rebekah. The throb in her forehead made reasoning difficult. How could her father accept an offer of marriage for her from a man so aged? A man whose own sons had taunted her in the temple? Her father would have refused Azor if she was not cursed.

Water boiled in the pot, waiting for new figs. She shut her eyes and prayed. *Give me wisdom, Lord. If Azor is my future, why do I only dream of Gil? He showed me kindness and treated me honorably.*

She stirred the figs and thought of her future, of the alley, of Gil. If she was to be healed and open to other offers of marriage, she would have to seek the prophet on her own. But how? The man of God had not returned to Jerusalem. Her father and brother grumbled at the fact that the prophet remained in Mahanaim, in the home of a wealthy landowner.

Traveling north to the border without an escort would cause more scandal to her reputation, more so than her curse. If indeed her father was entering her into a marriage contract with Azor, none of her family members would dare challenge his decision and help her escape. Only one man was bold enough to stand up to her brother. Her blood pounded through her veins as she recalled Gilead's strength. Was Gil brazen enough to help her flee the city? Would he travel with her to Mahanaim? Would he brave the scandal for her?

With a rag-draped hand, Hannah lifted the pot from the fire.

The harvest was ending. Gil would not be needed

in the fields. If they left soon, she could be healed and left free to petition her father for another husband before he exchanged sandals with Azor and sealed her fate.

"I need to go to the market." The words flew from Hannah's lips. "My family shall not want of fig cakes."

"The sun is still high. Can it not wait?" Rebekah said with discomfort in her voice.

Oh sister, if you only knew how much it cannot wait.

"There is a merchant who sells to…who will sell me honey."

"Make haste," her aunt added. "Your mother's prayers will end soon."

Hannah beheld her aunt's gaze. "I know my place."

After walking at a slow pace until she was a few houses from her own, Hannah raced down an alley toward the marketplace near where she had met Gil. Vendors called to her as she passed by, oblivious to who was behind the head covering. She had no time to tarry. A woman stepped into her path blocking her passage.

"*Tova.* Good," the woman declared, holding a leek up to Hannah's nose.

Hannah jerked away. There was no way she would know if the woman's offering was good or not. All food tasted like the wind.

The woman stepped back and gasped.

Hannah shielded her face and ran between two men bartering over spices. She scanned the sides of the street as she milled between buyers and sellers.

A few sheets dried in the sun, lining the street. Would she recognize Gilead's alcove? She peeked behind billowing blankets and between houses trying to find the right alley. Gilead's room. She stopped for a moment and rubbed her throat, smothering the fire that burned within. As she gasped for air, she studied the buildings ahead. The yellow hue of a sheet caught her attention. Either the woman of the home did not know how to keep house or the sheet had stayed up longer than an hour.

She jogged toward the familiar house with the high window, certain Gil lived under its sill. Ready to whip back the cloth and make a bold entrance, she hesitated. What if Gil wasn't alone? What if he didn't remember her?

Carefully, she pulled back the edge of the sheet ready to release it in a hurry if need be.

The crates were there.

The barrel was there.

Gil was not there.

Her shoulders slumped like each one held a jug of water. Where was Gil? In the fields? She knew he worked for a landowner but she didn't know which one. Neither time, nor her safety, would allow a trip out of the city.

Voices grew louder from the window above where Gil slept. A vision of Gil's mother yelling his name down the street filled her head. Would Gil's mother know when he would return?

She rushed to the doorway. Her tongue swept over her teeth, wetting her mouth.

Tap. Tap. Tap.

She waited.

Answer. Please. She knew someone was home.

The door cracked open. Hannah rubbed her palms together smoothing the moisture over her skin. She bowed her head and held her covering taut against her

15

face. "Greetings."

A woman stepped outside, a woman younger than Hannah imagined Gil's mother should be. Did Gil have an older sister?

The woman studied Hannah's sandals, woven belt, and embroidered head covering. Her brown eyes blinked as if she had been caught in a dust storm.

"*Shalom*," Hannah said softly. "I am in need of Gilead. Is he your son?"

The woman pressed forward, glancing back into the house before shutting the door.

"I cannot help you," she whispered. "I know little of my son's whereabouts."

Hannah bit her lip to keep from weeping. She was a fool to think her plans would be fruitful. God had cursed her. Her own people shunned her. Even Gil's mother refused her.

"Daughter." Gil's mother brushed her hand against Hannah's cheek. "My son is a good man. If you have need of him, he will find you."

"But how—"

A man bellowed from within the house.

"Shhh." The woman's eyes widened. "I must go."

"May I leave word?" The door closed before Hannah's request could enter. Hannah wondered if a life with Azor would be filled with such worry. Not ever speaking of her past or of her curses.

Turning the corner into Gil's alcove, she collapsed beside the barrel where she had taken refuge before. "Come to me Gil," she breathed. "Did you not speak of hope and mercy?" Her chest constricted as if the bronze hoops of the barrel had bound her ribs.

Her head snapped up on occasion when men's voices neared the sheet. But Gil's boisterous laugh never came. Her prayer had fallen on deaf ears. Again. The Jews were God's chosen people, but God had chosen to shun her. Punish her for something that happened long ago by an unknown ancestor. Perhaps Azor was all she deserved.

She had to get home. Her mother would return soon from the tabernacle. As she pushed herself up with the palm of her hand, her ruby bracelet settled on her wrist. She had not removed it in hopes the prophet would seek her out when he came to the temple. But the prophet lingered in Mahanaim instead of Jerusalem.

Balling her fist, she flayed at the side wall of Gil's house. The prophet's refusal to heal her had been the worst day of her life, but this day was in ruins as well. Burnt meals. Secret betrothals. No rescuer.

The sheet billowed in a gust of wind. Did it, too, rejoice in mocking her? A flash of rebellion tensed her body. She was tempted to rip down that soiled sheet. She lifted her hand to catch the frolicking cloth. The glimmer of her jeweled bracelet stopped her. Gil had seen the bracelet, commented on its value. He would remember it belonged to her. He would know she had visited his…she would not say it. She would not say bed.

Thieves could easily steal from Gil's alley. The alcove had few places to hide her bracelet. Gil's mother did not seem surprised by an inquiry about her son. An inquiry from a stranger. A woman in need. Did other women clamor to his door?

She stared at the barrel and decided it was a better fit than the crates with all their slats. She laid the circle of gold and rubies in the dust, in plain view from where Gil slept. Closing her eyes, she willed Gil to find the treasure, to find her.

She sprinted home, past the market, the well, the crowds.

Panting, she caught her breath before entering her home. Her mother stood near the pot of figs, ladle in hand, sampling the stewed fruit.

"It is sweet enough, Daughter."

Hannah nodded, her mind blank of a response. At least she had finally done one thing as planned today. But she did not plan on marrying a shriveled Levite. Her flesh itched at the thought of sharing a marriage bed with an old priest when all she could think about was sharing another moment with Gil. Seeking the prophet was her only hope of escape. The man of God had to set her free this time. Set her free from this sin stain. Set her free her from bondage to Azor. Set her free to be with a man like Gil.

Gil had to find the bracelet and come to her.

He had to.

She needed an escort out of the city and to Mahanaim. And Gil was the only man she could trust to take her.

3

All evening, Hannah wrestled with her bed sheet. Did Gil return home each night, or did he slumber in the fields? Would he spy her bracelet before a thief? Thoughts and schemes raced through her mind. When morning came, she hurried to her tasks, hoping chores would keep her sane.

She hoisted a water jar onto her shoulders, rushed out of the courtyard, marched to the well, and ignored the chatter of the women in line behind her. She wanted to proclaim, "I am not unclean. My father has made atonement." But would they even believe her?

As she returned home, a donkey loaded with bundled wheat shafts slowed the pace on the city street. She was caught in a crowd. Nestling the side of her face against the coolness of the clay jar, she hoped the drape of her head covering cloaked her from being recognized.

"Alabaster, beads, bangles," a merchant shouted.

Leave it to a salesman to find opportunity behind the rump of a slow donkey. His father had taught him well.

The chants of the merchant grew louder, came closer. "Men, trinkets for the fair and lovely."

Hannah believed the heckler was upon her. Did he mistake her for a man? She had no free hand to test his wares.

"Young woman."

The address was too close to ignore. Her elbow rose to ward off his seller's assault. Her heart rapped against her chest anticipating a run home.

"Ah, but your arm is bare. Can I not interest you in—"

She whipped her head his direction.

And stared.

At her bracelet. The rubies sparkled in the sunlight they captured.

At Gil. And his radiant smile.

"You do have interest." He herded her without a touch toward a narrow side street. "Your father has coin, no doubt."

She matched his pace not knowing where he was guiding her and not caring. Gil had found her and she would follow him out of the crowd, out of the city, out to Mahanaim. "You came."

He drew her into a doorway. The bustle of the city was but a memory. "Jewels are my business," he said in a loud voice. And lower, "My mother spoke of a sad girl in need. I know very few who wear such wealth." He held up her gold and ruby bracelet.

Setting her jar out of the way, she met his gaze. He grinned as if she had bought all his trinkets.

She let him take her arm and slip the bracelet on her wrist. His calloused fingers slid over her skin like a silk ribbon.

"It is a perfect fit," he said, eyeing a passerby. His fingers cocooned her hand and wrist.

"We are in public," she whispered.

"Did I not say it was lovely?" He winked and dared her with his just-made-a-sale eyes. How could she chastise him further when he was one of the few people who braved a touch?

He shifted closer. "What else do you have need of?" His tone was that of a true merchant.

You. She swallowed hard trying to figure out how to tell him of her true need. Her heart skittered like a startled rabbit in the wilderness. "The prophet is in Mahanaim." She took a deep breath. "I need to go to him."

He studied her face. His head dipped to the side as if he understood her request. "What of your brother?" His deep voice brimmed with curiosity and caution. He was still playing the role of the persistent merchant.

She shook her head. "Me. Solely, me."

His brows furrowed at her answer.

"I must go soon." She emphasized the last word.

Gil surveyed the street. His grip on her hand tightened. He must have determined no one was watching their interaction. The touch of his hand warmed her belly.

"Why the rush to see the prophet? Will he not return to the temple here?"

Her lips quivered with the answer. The emotion of her response pounded in her forehead, her throat, her chest. "My father has washed his hands of me. He is arranging my union to a priest."

"You are betrothed?" The words rasped from Gil's throat. He tore his hand away. "That is why your brother scolded me?"

"No. I do not think he knew. I did not know. My aunt spoke freely of it yesterday. She thought I knew of my father's decision." She wrapped her arms tight around her, keeping the shakes from racking her body.

Gil's stance mirrored hers. He lost the fervor of a merchant. He lost his words. His boisterous mannerisms vanished.

"I cannot blame my father. He has made every sacrifice to cleanse me. He brought me before the prophet. The year of Jubilee has passed me by. I am still in debt to this curse. My father accepted an honorable man's offer of marriage. A joining with a Levite."

"If he is an acceptable husband, why do you flee?" Gil leaned in to hear her slightest whisper.

She glanced away from him, toward the light above the sandstone buildings. Tears amassed behind her eyes. After a quick check of her surroundings, she grasped his hand and curled it in hers, resting it below her chin as a most cherished possession. "I want to be whole. Clean. A prize to my betrothed. Not a shackle." She spoke as if she had known Gil from the cradle. "That is why I need to see the prophet of Israel."

"For this priest?" He began to pull away.

"No." She held him fast, not wanting him to abandon her. If only she could confess that it was for him, the man who sought her out when others kept her at a distance, but giving him hope that they could be together was foolishness. "I do it for myself." She glanced downward at their intertwined fingers, at her sandal straps, anywhere but his handsome face. *God of Israel, listen to my heart.*

"There is nothing wrong with you." Gil lowered his face so she could not avoid his gaze.

"There is," she blurted out. "And I cannot lie to you. I carry a curse. Punishment for an ancestor's transgression."

He did not flinch. Her confession hung in the air, but he did not retreat in disgust.

She cherished the drag of his fingers over her

palm.

Gil held her hand close and captive and leaned closer. His free hand slid down her spine. "A tail? An extra leg?"

She jumped backwards cautioning him not to move his hand any lower.

Gil halted his tease.

"I have laid plans to disobey my father," Hannah said. "If I break any more laws, my intended may prefer another."

Gil gave a carefree laugh. "You are young and beautiful," he said in a low rumble of a voice. "Your intended will receive you as long as you remain a virgin."

Her back straightened. "I will remain a virgin."

"Come." Gil pulled her into the street.

"Where are we going?"

"I will escort you home." He gestured as a merchant showing a table of wares.

"Home?" Had he too decided to desert her?

"Your father owes me payment, does he not?" He cocked his head, expecting her to answer. "Do not worry," he whispered. "We will go north and find the prophet. What's one more commandment broken?"

Her eyes flew open wide. Had they broken God's laws? She had deceived, but did she lie? Had Gil? They had not committed adultery, unless…did he lust after her when he touched her? Was he coveting what was to be Azor's? Did she look to Gil as to a husband? Her bones became light as dust. Her mind raced. Gil was still speaking.

"Be like spies…sneak together…tonight."

She held onto her jar as onto a boulder in a swift running river. They were about to shatter a few commandments and her limbs were all a tingle.

4

Hannah tugged at the hood of her cloak to make sure it shaded her face. The loose fit of the garment hid her curves but didn't cover her guilt at leaving her family. How would her mother fare when in the dawn's light she would discover her only daughter had vanished, a ruby bracelet left in her stead? No robber would take a girl and leave gold. Her mother would know she had fled of her own free will.

She slid along a line of neighboring houses, her hand steadying herself against the ridged bricks in the early morning darkness. Air settled in her lungs like bundles of harvested flax, forcing her to choke out every breath. She moved discreetly toward the Dung Gate and let the woven layers of her linen tunic brush down to her toes, to shield her from the notice of the men carousing in the city after dark.

Her heart pulsed in her ears: Go back. Go back. Go back. But she would not obey. Every step brought her closer to being restored, made new. Her senses would be able to taste roasted quail or delight in the aroma of henna blossoms.

"*Shalom,*" a deep voice greeted.

She gasped. Alarm speared through her body. Her hand shot to her throat as she turned around. Her shoulders collapsed when she recognized Gil.

"You gave me no warning." Her words ached in

her throat.

"Did you forget our meeting place at the bend near the pools?"

Blinking, she scanned the area. "I did not realize I had arrived. My mind is awash with other things."

"Your family?" Gil's head bent lower. "You could wait. The prophet will return to Jerusalem, the city of David."

"When? How long must I suffer and wait?" She tucked loose strands of hair under her covering. "It is best I leave. My father cannot give away what he does not have. I do not want to be buried in the arms of an old widower." She looked at Gil, trying to see his expression in the shadows. Did he desire to stay in the fields? Did he have to protect his mother? Did he have misgivings? She cupped her hands but not in prayer. "Am I asking too much of you?" she stammered. "The fields—"

"Shhh." Gil hushed her worries and took hold of her arm, leading her toward the wall of the city. "The harvest has ended for me. My mother has her husband, his children. And I will have you back before we are missed."

"But what if we are seen? My parents are reasonable. Not so much my brother. They will not forgive you if they find out we have been alone together at night. My brother believes this curse is my fault."

"I will take the blame." Gil's voice did not waver. "Men from the tribe of Judah do not run from a fight."

"Neither do Levite women dressed as men." Her fists relaxed at Gil's quiet chuckle.

When his laughter died down, he met her gaze full on. "I, too, have reasons for wanting to see the prophet."

"Is your mother in need?" A rush of sympathy shortened her steps.

"Not of healing. If the prophet speaks for our God and does His will—"

"You know he does." Her words almost shrieked at his blasphemy.

"Then why is the daughter of the chief priest not healed? If you cannot be restored, what of the poor? The half-breeds?" Gil's pace quickened. They turned a corner.

"He said it was not my time."

Gil let out a low, breathy cough. "Has the prophet ever left a cripple maimed?"

She thought of all the times her father had spoken of the prophet's miracles. Miracles of their God. She could not remember a time when her father had come home disappointed. Well, there had been one time.

Gil broke the silence. "That is why I go. To see the man of God heal you or explain his failing. Why are some in Israel forgotten?" He halted as they neared the city wall. "I will accept nothing less than a full healing."

The sincerity and determination in his voice renewed her spirit. "Nor will I."

Gil stopped at an inn built into the wall of the city. He leaned his shoulder against the wooden planks of the door, and with an upward thrust of his body, opened the door without summoning the innkeeper. He led her through a tidy sitting area and a dish-stacked kitchen. People had gathered here, but they were asleep now. She followed him up a flight of stairs. Gil needed no lamp to light the way.

"You have been here before," she said, a bit

breathless. She wasn't sure if it was a statement of the truth or a question. She did not know if she wanted an answer.

"Yes, but not for a while." His voice wasn't even winded.

She and Gil scaled another set of stairs and then climbed a ladder leading to a small room. He hesitated in front of a window, an opening in the city wall framing the black of night. "We can drop down from here and be outside the city. We will be long gone before the gates open in the morning."

"Is it safe?" She had heard of thieves hiding in the hills.

"I have done it many times before."

"The innkeeper does not mind you coming and going?" She tried to spy the distance to the ground, but in the darkness it looked like a pit.

"Not if I share my winnings." His deep voice rattled low with a laugh. "Are you scared or curious about my ways?"

A little of both. She had never been alone with a man who wasn't a relative. She had not questioned Gil about the women he met in the gleaning fields or the women who hung out at night in the alleys, but now she wondered if he searched them out. "I do not leave the house after dark. My father says it tempts danger."

"Do not worry. No harm will come to you." Gil unhooked a coil of rope hanging near the window. "I don't sleep much." He handed her the end of the rope. "If I'm restless, I find a game of chance or drunkards to fool."

He opened a cupboard and withdrew a long, narrow sack. Even with only the moon's light, the outline was unmistakable. It was a sword.

"I won this casting lots." He fastened the blade to his belt as if it were nothing but a pouch of coins. "Perhaps the heavens knew I would have need of it." His hand grasped her arm, gentle but firm. "Come. I will lower you down."

She took the rope. The knotted cord stuck to her clammy palms. The frayed edge pricked her skin. Was this a warning about leaving home? Once she left Jerusalem, there was no turning back. She wrapped the rope around her waist, but fumbled the first twine.

"Here. Let me take care of this." Gil cinched the rope—not too tight—around her waist.

"That's what you do isn't it? Care for women and children in the gleaning fields. Keep them safe."

"I try." He helped her onto the sill. "In a few fields. Not all the women stay safe."

"Is that why you bring such a sword?"

"Mahanaim is near the border. The Ammonites do not concern me. They are weak. But Aram plunders our people. Wealth is their god. "

"We are not at war."

"The foreigners in the fields would disagree." He urged her forward and looped the rope through a pulley. "We must hurry."

Hannah gripped the cut stone of the sill. Her fingers grew warm from the tepid bricks hoarding the warmth from yesterday's sun. She turned, and braced her sandals against the wall. Sure of hand, she held onto the length of rope. She walked downward. Toe. Heel. Toe. Heel. The wall was her road. Gil lowered her, skillfully, carefully. The thud of her feet on solid ground released a gust of breath from her lungs. She unfastened the rope so Gil could join her in the wilderness. The knot she unbound seemed to take hold in her stomach.

A slight breeze blew against the side of her face. *Make haste.*

Gil scaled the wall with ease. The load he carried—sword, satchel, waterskin—did not impede his descent. He heaved the rope to the ledge with the skill of a herdsman.

"The innkeeper will know we have fled." She bit her lip in anticipation of word getting back to her family.

"I am not the only one who ventures from this window. I tied the knots of a fisherman not a field guard." He placed a hand on her swathed shoulders and guided her toward the path.

She should scold his touch. "Gi—"

"Save your breath daughter of Zebula. My thoughts are on what lays ahead, not what lies beneath. We must put distance between us and Jerusalem."

Even if he was being untruthful, she would not remove his hand. The weight was comforting and no one could see. No one could gossip.

After they had walked a few miles, Gil bartered for a ride on the back of a wagon stacked with bird cages. Were these fowl for sin offerings? Perhaps the man bred them for sale? She was too tired to ask. She dangled her legs off the rear of the cart as Gil steadied the wheels. Blood pulsed through her throbbing toes. The birds didn't seem to mind the jolts and jostling from the rocky terrain, but her feet minded the bruising rocks. The bounce of the wagon eventually lulled her to sleep. Her head bobbed and bobbed and bobbed. Each stone they crossed seemed as big as a boulder.

Doves cooed.

Pigeons rooted.

She pitched forward.

"Lean on me." Gil drew her closer to his side.

She stiffened. *We shouldn't be this close. Thank goodness for my extra layers of clothing.*

"No one can see us," he whispered as if he could read her thoughts.

How much time had passed? The last she remembered, Gil was overseeing the cart's wheels. His arm rested between her back and the cages, anchoring her body to the boards. She looked around. No one walked nearby. His embrace was well hidden. It kept her from falling.

She blinked at the fresh sun, a thin amber ribbon draped over the hilltops.

"My parents will discover I am gone soon." She shielded her eyes. "My mother will weep."

Gil loosened his hold. "We could turn around." He squinted at the sunrise and opened his satchel.

If they returned now, Gil's life would not change, but she would be considered tainted, a shame her father's position could not erase. Not even Azor would have her. But when the prophet healed her, made her new, all her transgressions would be forgiven.

"No. This is the path I have chosen. I want to be whole." A row of ruts in the ground caused the birds to squawk. Hannah righted one of the cages. "My father has sacrificed doves for my cleansing." She smiled as though her condition were commonplace. "It didn't work. Nothing has."

Gil's gaze made her uncomfortable.

"The first time we met, I gave you some pomegranate."

Hannah nodded. "You called it your sweet delight."

"It wasn't ripe. Sour enough to pucker your lips."

Her lap held her interest. Had he realized her mouth was dead? Had he known all along?

"I'm a poor judge of food." She fiddled with her head covering, pulling it tight to her face. Had he seen her ear stubs while she rested? "When I met your mother, I had burned a pot of figs."

He seemed amused. "I cook. I can take care of us." He untied a cloth and offered it up to her. "Have some dried mutton?"

Her stomach growled its approval. She bit into the dried meat and contemplated her companion. Walking half the night and being dusted face to toe didn't seem to drain his spirit. He already knew of her father and brother, of the temple rituals, of her curse. But stories about his family never surfaced in conversation. "Have you worked in the fields long?"

Gil stroked his bearded chin. He seemed older, fatigued in some way.

"Since I grew into my height and learned to fight." Gil looked at the caged birds as though he heard their ruckus for the first time.

"Do you still have to fight?"

"Sometimes…if the bandits have not heard of my reputation." He flipped the hood of her cloak over her covering so it shielded her face. "And I don't want to be challenged this early in the morning." He grinned and popped a piece of mutton into his mouth. "Can't protect you on a hollow stomach."

"Surely not." She accepted another strip of meat. Maybe it would settle her stomach. Her insides trembled as if the donkeys were at a full trot. Was it his

32

proximity, or the pain she heard in his voice when he spoke of the fields? Her shoulders slumped under the weight of her secret. He had left his position, his home, and his family to escort a stranger. He deserved to know the truth about her.

She rubbed her hands together, loosening salt grains from the meal. "I cannot taste your mutton. I cannot taste anything." Warmth spread into her cheeks, up into her scalp.

"That is all?"

Did he understand what she had revealed? A shiver sliced through her, cooling her skin. She had disobeyed her father's command not to reveal her secrets. She had revealed one.

"I figured as much," Gil said. "My mouth was as tight as a drawstring after tasting that pomegranate." He tilted her chin toward his face. "And your eyes are not watering. My mutton is flavored with spices from the east. No one begs me for a bite."

She instinctively licked her teeth. But still, nothing. Gil didn't seem to care. If he did, he hid it well. He sat, his leg still aligned with hers, still touching hers. Tears pooled behind her eyes. "I do not know what the world smells like. These birds and their droppings are nothing to me. My nose is like wood." Her throat tightened.

He swallowed his last bite of mutton. "Then you may sit downwind." His light-hearted laugh mixed with the coo-cooing cadence of the birds.

Stunned, she stared at him. The prophet had humiliated her. A future with an elderly priest awaited her. How could he tease her? Turning away, she gripped the edge of the cart.

Gil hopped off the back of the wagon. He faced

her as he kept pace with the wheels. "I do not laugh at you. I laugh at those who scorn a woman like you. You eat and breathe. You are not lame or blind or demon possessed. I was dirty from the fields, and you treated me with respect. Why should you not seek it for yourself?"

Did he think her acceptable? He hadn't seen her deformity.

"I'll be stopping in Jericho to rest the animals," the bird owner interrupted. "I will need help in crossing the Jordan. If you can guide the donkeys with me, you and your wife may ride on farther. Your wife can secure the cages."

"My wife and I are in your debt," Gil shouted.

Hannah's mouth fell open. "You should not support this lie," she whispered.

"If we tell him we are not bound together, he would not have us for sure." The breath of his words tickled her cheek. "Only a fool would deny that he is your husband. And it will cause us more trouble if he thinks you will leave one man for another."

He was correct. She was cursed, but not by her own doing. There was no way she would allow herself to be branded as a traveling prostitute.

"I trust you are good with livestock, Husband."

5

North of the River Jabbok, they camped for the night. She brought Gil a cup of water, wanting nothing more than to stay on watch with him, but she wasn't truly his wife, the one blessed to benefit from his warmth at night. Gil paced by a large rock sheltering the wagon and readied his sword to protect their one-cart caravan from bands of Arameans daring to cross the border or a desperate thief in need of sacrificial fowl.

The snores of the bird merchant relayed his trust of Gil. Awash in muddy water, Gil had driven the donkeys to shore hours before, never a complaint or a curse.

"Do not think ill of me." Gil accepted her cup. His brown eyes were as serious as she had ever seen them. "I follow our laws, the laws of Moses. I lied today for your protection."

"I know." She stepped close enough to smooth the furrow in his brow. She would not condemn her rescuer. Not now. Not ever. "You are an honorable man."

"And you are my temptress. That is another reason why I came."

She stepped back, her tongue unable to form a response.

"I cannot lie anymore today." He gulped the

water.

"Your truth is my truth." She spoke honestly. Her testimony left her lightheaded and weak legged. *Will he still care for me if he sees my deformity?* She truly hoped so, for her feelings for Gil had taken root and formed buds.

"Go lay in the cart." Gil's command held a hint of amusement. "Mahanaim is another day's journey. Soon, the man of God will receive us."

"I will recline but I do not know if I will sleep." She took the cup from him. "May you find some rest this night."

He tested the sheath of his sword. "As you wish. Though, it is unlikely." The gravelly rasp of his voice left a deepening ache in her soul.

The warped planks of the wagon did not encourage her sleep. When she thought of demanding an audience with the prophet, her blood raced through her veins, swift and surging, like the waters of the Jordan during a flood. Sweat moistened her scalp. It was not the desert heat that tormented her but fear of the prophet's refusal, fear of parting from Gil, fear she would be trapped in a betrothal with Azor. The betrothal she desired was to the man who guarded her safety a few feet away.

That afternoon, the merchant left them a short journey from Mahanaim while he and his birds headed north to the Yarmuk River. She and Gil walked east, to the lands of another Levite clan, to the prophet's preferred residence.

Gil inhaled deeply. "Sheep. There must be a herd nearby."

"We are fortunate you can smell them."

"I'm not." He turned and strode backward, eyeing

her gait. "We could use shelter and a rest."

She lengthened her stride. "If you must."

Halting at the edge of a plateau, she and Gil scanned a valley and noticed a sprawling village. Olive groves and animals took nourishment from the fertile soil between the rugged cliffs.

Gil's pace quickened. "Come. The valleys of Manasseh are not far from Mahanaim. I have heard talk of their bounty."

Hannah lifted her face to the sun. Its rays seemed brighter as she grew near to her destination. She followed Gil down the slope. Her arms swung wildly as if she had wings and could fly into the valley, taking Gil with her in one glorious swoop. Elation overcame her. She remembered the same feeling of joy when her father had slipped the ruby bracelet on her arm and proclaimed that the prophet would have her unshackled from her curse by noonday. Her heart pained when she pictured leaving the ruby bracelet by her sleeping mother and slipping into the night to meet Gil.

When they reached the rows of olive trees, she walked next to the grooved trunks, relishing the shade and closeness to Gil.

She picked up a leafy branch from the ground and used it as a fan. "Perhaps we will find some ripe pomegranates in the village."

"You have tired of my mutton?"

"Mostly of my bread. It is as hard as this." She tried to snap the olive twig but it bent instead.

Gil broke off the end and handed it back to her. "You will be able to taste how sweet the fruit is after you are healed."

"We can both sing praises of *Selah*." She bowed in

jest, making sure he did not see that there was more to her healing than of what she had already spoken. She let out a silly laugh.

A flock of ravens shot heavenward, darkening the sky, cawing in protest. Did the playful noise disturb their rest?

The ground trembled.

She looked to Gil. Was it an earthquake?

Dust rolled through the grove like it was driven by a windstorm. But there was little to no wind. Not a breeze that would ruffle a skirt.

In the next lane of trees, a shepherd boy raced by them. "*Ratz!* Run," he shouted, his voice shrill with panic.

Gil stiffened. He grew to his full height, let go of her hand, and reached for his sword.

"Run." He pushed her in the direction of the shepherd, of the buildings they had passed.

Hannah glanced over her shoulder.

Hoof beats thundered in her ears. Shouts. Sheep bleating. Foreign gibberish. .

She grasped Gil's arm. "Come with me."

"Go." He shoved her—hard. "Please, Hannah. Hide."

How could she abandon him? She couldn't. Blood pounded in her temples. She choked out a refusal.

"I won't watch you die or worse." His shouts pained her ears. He stiff-armed her in the direction they had come.

She shook her head, "Ple—"

"Now! *Ratz!*" he screamed.

He didn't have to scream twice. She fled. She left Gil. Left him alone to face the danger.

Fear propelled her down the path. Her feet

pounded the dirt but her legs lightened as if they were empty, filled only with wind. She bunched up her cloak to keep herself from stumbling. Gil needed assistance and she would find help.

"Thieves are upon us," she yelled as she neared a village.

A sound like an avalanche of rocks muffled her warning. She whipped around. Across the field, she saw horses stampede forth from the olive trees. Men in breastplates with arms-length swords slashed at wayward livestock, slicing them in half with their weapons.

People appeared from the stable, from the houses, from the garden, ignorant of the ensuing battle.

"Raiders," she screamed. "Enemies."

A man stood in her path. His eyes were wide and his jaw gaped.

"Grab a weapon. Fight," she urged, gasping for air.

The man pushed her aside and fled toward town.

She followed him and darted into a stable. Stripping off her outer garment, she fumbled for her father's carving knife. The clop of horses' hooves grew louder. Her lungs seemed too small to hold the air she needed. Her chest shuddered. She coughed and ducked under a window, crawling behind bales of hay stacked in the shadowy corner of the barn. The day filled with shrieks, familiar and foreign. She thought of Gil defending himself against the charge and sank to her knees and prayed. *Adonai, spare my Gilead.*

Curled in a ball, she waited.

Creeeaaak.

The stable door whined as it opened. A sliver of light slipped between the bales. A horse neighed.

Straw crunched beneath footsteps. The foot falls came closer. Hannah held her breath.

A man called out. She did not understand his words. One word, in Aramaic, she recognized. He was indicating a stallion.

Her heart crashed against her ribs, sending jolts of pain across her chest. She staggered her breathing and tried to be silent, undetected.

Horses clopped out of the building. The shuffling of feet stopped. So did the mumbling of voices. The stable door slammed shut. She remained untouched. Sinking into the brittle bales, she thanked God she wasn't beaten, bloodied, or badly used.

Peeking out from the wall of hay, she grasped a small paring knife and prowled toward the stable door. She listened. A woman sobbed in the distance, but on the street, there was no uproar. She had to find Gil. Dead or alive, she needed to be with him.

She opened the door the width of her foot, no more.

A face appeared. Male. Dark. Sweating. Bloody.

She inhaled. The man clamped a hand around her throat. Her vision blurred and she lurched forward, struggling to breathe.

Stab him. Hit him. Hit something.

She thrust the knife forward.

The tip of her blade struck bronze. A club struck her fist. Fire burned in her bones. Her fingers splayed in agony and her knife dropped. The man dragged her into the street.

"No. No. No." Kicking, she fought her abductor. "Leave me be."

The man mocked her in a tongue she barely recognized. He raised the club.

Bhaamp.

Her vision sparkled with graying sunbursts. *Will I see Gil in death?*

Then darkness fell.

6

The trot of a horse jostled her awake. Her ears thrummed with an echo like the summons of a far off ram's horn. The wet withers of a horse glimmered below her chest, arms, and bound hands. Her stomach burned from being flung across the shoulders of a bobbing animal. She could not flail her legs. Her thighs were pressed together. Her ankles were probably bound as well.

She struggled to raise her head and get her bearings despite the pulsing, painful rhythm in her temples. Her head covering was gone. No cloth hid her foul ears. The sun tormented her flesh without it.

Reins cracked against her backside. She flinched. Her flesh stung, sizzling at first and then waning to a throb. A man's voice spoke. The language was strange, sprinkled with words one hears in trade. His blunt, hard laugh ricocheted between her ears.

"The Hebrew coward awakes."

She understood his insult, not his dialect. His common Aramaic was crude. She shifted and twisted her neck to view her captor. He was one of the eastern peoples. He sat tall on the horse. His broad, armor-adorned body blocked the sun just enough for her to scan his sharp, angular face. Blood spotted the bridge of his nose and above his brow. Was it hers? Or Gil's?

His hand slipped between her thighs. "Are you

anxious?"

Her back went rigid. Her shoulders shook with a chill. She would not let this heathen raider take her virginity. She had to escape and find Gil. Rocking her body side-to-side, slamming into the rider's thighs, she prayed the *Shema.*

"Hear, O Israel: The Lord is our God, the Lord alone. Love—"

He removed his hand.

She blew out a pent up breath. *Shalom, Adonai.*

An all-out gallop silenced her holy prayer. Dust embedded in her eyes, churned up from the pounding hooves. Each bounce of the horse's cantor bruised her belly, and by the time tents came into view, she swore she had been disemboweled. At a fevered pace, she worked her wrists against the scratchy rope in hopes of loosening the knots before her captor fondled her body with fervor.

A forceful push on her hip sent her careening head first toward the ground.

Air gusted from her lungs. The stallion pranced. It side-shifted its hooves away from her neck and head. At least one thing had gone right today.

With a quick glance around, she noticed she was in a valley. High cliffs. High caves. No shade. Many tents. No sign of Gil. No sign of other captives.

Footsteps crunched the pebbled ground. Her captor barked commands at soldiers standing nearby. Grumbling protests followed.

She rolled on her back and faced her abductor. He licked his lips, rustling the black hairs of a mustache that needed trimming. His mud-brown skin, ridged and worn from weather, was darker than hers. He was not a Hebrew.

"Let me go," she said, half in anger, half as a plea. "We are not at war."

He stared at her like she was a celebratory feast.

Her heart skittered, rallying a cry of run, run, run, run, run. "I have nothing to offer you."

The soldier's head rocked backward. A chest-jiggling cackle filled the air.

"Demands?" He knelt beside her, grinding her waist into the dirt with his knee. "You are a lowly slave. One who I see has been bad." His fingernails scratched her cheekbone as he gathered the hair away from her ear. "I shall take my pleasure."

He lifted her from the ground as if she were an empty sack and pinned her against the side of a plateau. Dirt crumbled from its base.

A blade flashed in the corner of her vision. She shut her eyes at its blinding reflection and dwelled on the sparkling bursts behind her eyelids. If only she could fly away into the light. The ropes binding her ankles loosened. Her skin breathed air.

He raised her hem, exposing her legs.

"No," she screamed, lurching forward.

"No one denies Konath." He pinned her with his chest, his armor warm and heavy. "You will serve me and then"—his hand fisted in her hair—"you will entertain my men."

She struggled. She had to get away. She would not be violated by a pagan. She flattened her bound hands against his breastplate and bowed her legs. Her heart pounded in protest, in utter disgust, in outrage, but she smiled wide like a barterer with flawed goods. The sides of her mouth trembled as he came in close. Too close. She jerked her knee upward like a battering ram of wrath.

He roared. Bent over. Covered his pain. His agony echoed through the camp.

She fled.

Toward the tents. Away from the soldiers and their horses. Away from the direction they had come.

She needed cover. A place to hide. But where? She passed stacks of wood, hanging animal carcasses, tents, and more tents.

Shouts sounded behind her. Konath was coming.

A large dwelling stood anchored at the edge of camp. Its flaps were tied. Did it house slaves? Spoils of war? Her bound hands fumbled with the knots. A buzzing blanket of horseflies bombarded her face. She whipped her hair around and wondered if there was a carcass or food inside. This refuge would only buy her time. She needed a miracle to escape Konath. And God remained silent.

She entered the muted shade of the shelter and drew the flaps flush as best she could. Turning to scour the contents of the room, movement caught her attention. She turned and cupped her mouth, suppressing a scream.

A man lounged on an ornate wooden chair. The exquisite carvings of petals and claws matched his decorated armor. His half-lidded eyes studied her from either side of an oozing sore. He had no nose. Only gaping, scarlet openings.

He pointed at her with a finger. His hand lacked others.

"Did you not smell the plague?" His tone held her in contempt. "The gnats hold court where I live."

Hannah dropped to her knees. She didn't know if she had done so willingly or if her knees had buckled. Her stomach heaved.

Konath called to his men from outside the tent.

Her rape was imminent.

"Have mercy on me." Her voice squeaked out among sobs and her body rocked like an inconsolable mourner. "We share a bond. We do. My nose is as worthless as yours. I cannot smell a thing."

The man's brow furrowed. Did he understand Hebrew? She began to speak in Aramaic.

He held up his fingerless hand. "I speak your language."

"My Lord Naabak, did a captive interrupt your rest?" Konath emphasized every word as if his superior was drunk or dumb. His loud cadence slithered like an asp over her shoulders. "Send her out for the sport of your men."

Hannah's body fell limp. She was the daughter of the chief priest, a descendant of the brother of Moses, but she was not too proud to crawl. She crawled toward this Naabak and latched onto his boot. The shoe caved. She flinched. No toes supported the leather. Her tears spotted the dust covered boot. She wiped the wetness with her hair not caring if her ears were bared. She doubted he had any ears left under his helmet.

"I beg you. Spare my honor." She slid her bound hands along the side of his boot and anchored herself to him. He did not pull away. They would have to pry her off of him. "I am the daughter of a priest. To die this way…as a whore…I cannot."

"I shall send in a soldier to remove her." Konath's voice rose with impatience, sounding uncertain, like he needed permission.

She hugged the ankle of the boot to her chest.

"She is within my control." Naabak called out. He

46

fidgeted in his chair, but did not pull his leg away from her. "She will stay with me for the evening."

Silence reigned outside the tent. Hannah wondered if she would meet the same fate inside the hide walls as outside, but then she remembered Naabak's leprous fingers.

"But Lord—"

Naabak bolted forward in his chair.

She huddled next to his feet.

"Am I not in command?" he shouted.

Konath did not reply.

"Post a guard if you like." Anger deflated from Naabak's voice.

The shuffle of footsteps and hushed murmurs waned.

"You." Naabak turned to address her. "How are you named?"

"I was given the name Hannah by my father, a Levite priest."

Naabak chuckled.

She did not look away, but beheld his deformity, picturing his face whole. He did not seem to be an unattractive man, but it was difficult to tell with blood and pus holding her focus.

"And my rot is acceptable to you?"

She hesitated. The years of keeping her secrets weighed on her conscience. Gil did not forsake her. Would this foreigner even care if she was stained by sin? Would he treat her differently if he knew she was cursed? She remembered the law: Thou shall not lie.

"My nose and mouth are—" She struggled to find an acceptable word. "Um...dead. They have been since birth. You are no different than any other to me."

"A benefit for you now, or you would not have

ventured into my dwelling. Only the flies clamor to get in."

"And my ears." She brushed back her hair. "Are like yours, I think. I can hear your words even though they are deformed. Sometimes I think God is laughing at me. My nose and mouth look fine, but do not work, and my ears work, but are maimed."

Naabak stared at the tent flap. His body went still as sculpted stone.

She rose and knelt on one knee. "I am indebted to you. You spared my life."

His expression hardened. "You may not survive a visit to this tent. It is afflicted with disease."

"What is one more curse compared to the rape of your men?"

"It is a slow death." Naabak warned of the suffering with his eyes.

She held his gaze. "Both would be a slow death for me."

Naabak grinned. "Ah, Israel you are bold. You approach me and speak as if we are known to each other. My household could use a slave who is not fearful of my decay."

Her lungs emptied of air. He had called her a slave. "But my home is in Jerusalem."

"Not anymore. I cannot deny my men and then give you freedom. You will be a gift to my wife. She is in need of a servant." He settled back against his upright bed. "There is a mat in the corner on which you can sleep tonight."

This could not be. Gil was taken from her and now her family? She collapsed as a wheat kernel smashed by a runner stone. She glanced toward the tent flap. An escape? She sighed. That would send her into the arms of Konath.

"But now I need to eat. Do you cook?"

She beheld Naabak's eyes. "Not well."

A deep, hearty laugh filled the warm air. "You and my wife." Liquid seeped from the open sore which was his nose. He hardly seemed to care.

He urged her forward and sliced the rope from her wrists with a silver-handled dagger. The tremor in his better hand caused her to utter another prayer.

"Cut a plum." He indicated a paring knife lying on a plank of wood.

"You trust me?" *With a weapon?*

"Do not worry. I am still strong enough to overcome you. If we wrestle, I do not need to kill you. The touch of my skin will."

She poured Naabak a cup of water and impaled pieces of fruit on a pronged stick. While she was already unclean from touching Naabak's leg, she would not tempt the infection by lingering at his mouth. She offered him food. "Are there other prisoners? Hebrew men?"

He chewed his plum. Her question seemed to mean nothing to him. To her it meant everything.

"Rarely. We have little need of farmers."

She stilled as her heart stuttered. Heat flushed her face. She did not mean for Gil to sacrifice his life. He was an escort to their prophet. She and Gil had walked on soil tread by Abraham and Moses. He was the first man who had accepted her. All of her. His touch sent her soaring to the heavens. She closed her eyes to calm the grief welling in her soul. Somehow she would see the prophet, even if it took years. Gil's death would not be in vain. She would not let him down.

"Israel."

Her eyes flew open. "Yes—" She swallowed hard. "Master."

"Do not bother to pack for me. When we leave for Damascus in the morning, it will all burn."

She nodded.

I already have left everything.

7

Twirling black billows of smoke rose into the early dawn sky, eager to overtake the hesitant sunrise. Hannah's eyes and nostrils burned as she watched the flames consume Naabak's dwelling.

A soldier shoved clothes in her direction. "Put these on. Throw your infected rags in the fire."

She took the tunic and tried not to think of how Konath and his men had come by it. At least there were no blood stains to remind her of its former owner.

The soldier did not move away. His gaze sat heavy on her breasts.

"Am I not afforded privacy? Hebrew women are taught to be modest."

"Mount up," Naabak shouted. He sat astride a horse with more armor than was owned by her whole clan of priests.

The soldier raced to obey Naabak's order, but she had traded an unknown set of eyes for Naabak's.

"Will you turn away, Master?" Respect filled her voice.

He hesitated.

"For your wife?" She appealed to his honor.

Turning his horse, he faced his men, keeping an acceptable distance for a leper.

She hid behind a donkey that was to be her mount and whipped off her clothes, covering her body before another Aramean could indulge his lust. The nightmare remembrance of Konath's hands on her thigh sent a shiver through her bones.

Sitting atop her donkey, traveling in the dust of her new master, she looked for Gil. But all she saw was his ghost. How could she, a cursed sinner, have lived and Gil have perished?

A full day of travel brought the caravan of soldiers and bleating livestock to a walled fortress set high on a stair-stepped cliff. The black-colored muzzles of sheep were now grayed with dust. Sweat dampened any cloth visible from under the soldier's chest plates. In the distance was the city of Damascus. She guessed the prominent gold-crested dome was where the king resided.

Naabak's armor bearer grabbed the mane of her donkey. "This way."

He led her across a field and down a stone street. All the while, she etched the landscape into her brain. She would venture this direction again. Alone. To freedom.

They stopped at a chiseled archway. The armor bearer shouted for her to dismount.

Hannah's thighs stiffened as her feet hit the ground. She hobbled up the steps into an entryway where a giant mosaic of a grand peacock greeted her. She traced the square-cut tiles of baked clay feeling as broken as the pottery. Was this the home of Naabak's wife?

Her guide left her to admire the art.

Run, she thought. But where?

Footsteps echoed on the clean-swept floor.

"A breathing, living gift."

The Aramaic greeting startled her. She whipped

around. A young woman draped from shoulder to ankle in indigo scarves stood before her. With gold filigree dangling from her ears and bathing her neck, this woman had to be Naabak's wife. A wife whose age matched Hannah's.

She dropped to her knees, straightening the borrowed tunic and adjusting her head covering.

"If I did not know of my husband's state, I would be jealous of how you spent last night."

"Of me?" How could this woman whose beauty shone like polished bronze be envious of a slave? A masterpiece of braided hair crowned the woman's head. Cascading ringlets, the color of onyx, complemented her dark skin. "I am least of all a temptress," Hannah offered.

"Hah. You could be. There is something hidden in your eyes that tantalizes even me, let alone a man. My husband must have seen something to offer you his protection." She grasped Hannah's arm and lifted her to her feet.

"I am to serve you, but I do not know what to do." Her gaze fell to the lady's polished toenails.

"Nothing. Until I give you a task. Now, tell me of my husband. Everything you observed. His face…"

Hannah looked into the tearful, curious eyes of her mistress. How did one describe a decaying husband to his wife?

"Your husband's face is…" She tried to find a word that would not get her beaten. "Worn." Unease tingled in her gut as she envisioned Naabak's deformities. "His nose is no more, but his hair is long and full."

"And his hands? Are they mostly whole?"

Hannah hesitated. Her mistress seemed eager for a

good report. She licked her cracked lips. Dry ridges of skin threatened to cut her tongue. How much should she share? The truth. She needed to gain this woman's trust. "I am afraid he has only a few fingers."

Naabak's wife stiffened as one told of death.

Will she punish me for my honesty?

"He keeps a distance from me. From everyone." The voice of her mistress was small and strained. "We had only shared the marriage bed for three weeks and then he fell ill. When you cannot touch one that is yours, it is easier to go off and fight. And fight well he does."

Hannah's heart hollowed. Naabak's prowess had claimed Gil's life.

"It is getting late. Follow me to my chamber." Naabak's wife indicated a staircase on the far side of the room, the opposite direction from which Hannah had come.

"Yes, Mistress." The title nagged at her conscience. She could hear her father's disdain. A Levite did not serve a pagan.

"In my home you will call me by my given name, Reumah."

"Is your family located here for me to serve?" Hannah tried to sound humble as she observed how many people she would have to slip past when she escaped.

Reumah gave a detached chuckle. "And chance the plague or a disgruntled spirit? My father received coin aplenty when I married, but all I received was isolation. What I wouldn't pledge for one more night of ecstasy to be filled with Naabak's heir. At least, then, my future would be certain."

And what of my future? I cannot stay in a foreign land

and worship foreign gods. "I was to attend a newborn in Jerusalem. Now I will serve you."

She followed Reumah up each stair. The lady lingered in her ascent as if each step moved her closer to the gallows. What rush was there for her mistress, she thought? She had no brother or child to attend. Near the top of the staircase, Hannah glanced out a window at the bustling of soldiers below. A town of canvas tents and mason-laid barracks dotted the plain, holding her interest.

A touch came upon her arm. In her exhaustion, she didn't remember how long she had been staring at the men scurrying outside.

"Only a fool would leave this house without an escort. The men respect my position and follow my letters. If you leave without protection, you would be theirs for the taking."

Hannah turned toward Reumah. "My life and my virginity are all that I have left, and that is due to your husband's mercy. He took pity on a poor prisoner."

"And he is not here." Reumah's brown-eyed gaze bore in on Hannah. "The ring where his men train is more suitable for him. If you see death every day, your own mortality becomes easier to bear."

"I don't believe death will ever be commonplace for me. When I saw death, I hid."

"You are Hebrew? Are you not? Do you not slaughter?"

A river of sparks sizzled to her fingertips. She breathed deeply and forced an ignorant smile. "I have seen the sacrifice of animals for cleansing, but not of people."

"Yes." Reumah's face lit with remembrance. "I have heard of that."

She followed Reumah down a hall until she stood before two mahogany doors carved in floor-to-ceiling vines. Hannah expected to see grape clusters hanging from the doorframe. When Reumah displayed the room, Hannah chuckled to herself to see cushions the color of celebratory wine.

The bed in the corner of the room beckoned to be noticed. A tapestry of scarlet, mustard, and green thread hung above a courtyard of pillows. Images of Gil flashed in her mind. She envisioned him coming through the door, grinning, ready to finish their journey. She missed his tender touches. His teasing. Her chest ached like someone squeezed her heart. Bending, she clutched a fist to her breast. .

"Are you ill?" Concern filled Reumah's voice.

Did the woman think she was succumbing to Naabak's leprosy? She would not be cast from this position as lowly as it was. "I was remembering someone I loved."

Reumah seemed relieved. She ushered Hannah over to a cedar table and acted as if they were relatives sitting down to discuss the day's news at the city gate.

"I have never known a man." Her cheeks warmed with her confession.

"But the man?" Reumah's eyes sparkled with interest.

"Is dead." She stroked the knot on her rationed belt. The garment's owner fared no better than Gil. Both had been slain in the promised land of God, but she was dragged to sinful soil. Would her curses never end?

"It's unfortunate good men die in battle." Reumah offered her a spoonful of honey from an alabaster jar. "Eat. It will brighten your eyes. I had some earlier today. It is the sweetest I have tasted in a long while."

"You are too kind to a foreigner." Hannah let the flattery slip from her tongue. Her gut tensed. *Gil did not die in a just war. He was trapped and murdered.*

She accepted the spoon and smacked her lips, swirling her tongue around her mouth like she could taste the thick liquid. She knew nothing of sweet or delectable. "I should be serving you."

"Oh, you will." Reumah placed the spoon back into the jar. "But you have seen my husband and Mereb has not."

"Mereb?" Hannah wondered who else was in the house.

"Another slave." Reumah glanced toward the door and then laughed. "He is an old Moabite. Time spent with him does not go swift."

Hannah eased back in her chair. Her master liked to talk. "Is your family far away?" All the better for Hannah if there were no guests coming and going from the house.

"They are behind the city walls, safe from the evil that has cursed my husband, and they believe, this household."

"Evil?"

"Naabak's plague." Reumah ran a finger around the lip of the honey jar. "Many fear our dwelling harbors evil spirits sent by angry gods." She licked her finger and raised her arms up in the air. "I see no spirits. Do you?"

"I know only of the God of Abraham. But I sense no spirits."

Reumah was a comely woman, attractive, not frothing at the mouth or clawing herself like a woman possessed by demons.

A knock on the door interrupted their conversation.

Reumah called for the person to enter.

A man hurried into the bed chamber. If this was Mereb, he was older than Hannah expected, or at least it was how he appeared. His skin was like raisins, almost black, and grooved—scarred perhaps. The turban on his head was spotless unlike Gil's earth-stained coils. How could Naabak trust a man, even an old one, around his attractive wife? Perhaps Mereb was a eunuch.

Reumah rose to her feet. "Oh, Mereb, can't I have one evening without you."

"A feast has been set for you, Mistress." He glanced at Hannah.

"My husband brought her to me." Reumah motioned for Hannah to stand. "You are not the only one who has escaped execution."

Mereb bowed to Reumah. "If Naabak has deemed her worthy of this position, then we will work as one." He turned to leave and motioned to Hannah to follow him.

Hannah rose and clasped her hands behind her back. She bowed before joining Mereb.

Reumah nodded. "The honey is at work already. I am certain."

Mereb closed the massive doors. "Is she ill?" he asked.

"Not that I noticed."

Hannah followed the Moabite down the hall. There were two small rooms at its end—barren squares containing a basket for clothes, a mat to lie on, and a bowl for waste. No doors. No secrecy. The close quarters reminded Hannah of the alcove where she had first met Gil. Her throat tightened as she remembered his carefree smile and bold laughter. If only he could visit this room, lie on her mat. She squeezed her eyes shut. She would not cry. She had to flatter Reumah and stay in her favor.

Collapsing onto the woven mat, Hannah pricked her lips with some stale bread portioned on a plate. How would she escape from Aram and return to her family? The daughter of Zebula was not born into slavery. She passed the evening listing what she would need for her journey—a horse, a skin of water, a weapon. How would she arrive at such a stash?

A squeeze to her shoulder sent her heart racing. She sprung into a seated position and came face to face with Mereb. "I thought someone had come to harm me."

Mereb let go of her shoulder. "There is no answer at our master's door. I fear for her. You said she was ill."

Had she? She stood and rubbed her arms, calming the bumps that had risen from her start. Mereb had mentioned Reumah's sickness. She was not the first. Was her mistress distraught at the report she had brought about Naabak?

She hurried down the hall to Reumah's bedchamber. There was no need to knock if Mereb had not received an answer. She pushed open the door. Perhaps Reumah had fainted?

Hannah sprinted into the room and a moan caught her attention. It came from the bed. She gasped and covered her mouth.

Reumah reclined on the bed, her head slung backward on a pillow. Konath lounged beside her.

8

Hannah turned and fled. Reumah's sultry pose, and the image of Konath gazing at her body, stunned Hannah's morality. Konath's wrath-filled eyes chilled her blood. She hesitated at the top of the stairs. Did she dare run down into the camp? No. She did not need a crowd of leering men to watch her punishment.

Racing to her room, she flattened her back against the wall and prayed the couple would return to their adultery.

Pounding footsteps echoed down the hallway. Konath was coming. Mereb had vanished. She tried to calm her breathing. Her chest burned for air. *God of Abraham, Isaac and Jacob, do not abandon me now.*

"You dog." Konath was upon her. He clenched her throat with calloused hands still warm from sin. "Forgetting your place has ruined my night."

Hannah's face grew hot. Her temples drummed a deafening beat. An apology gurgled in her voice box.

Konath relaxed his grip. She renewed her apology. He butted her head into the wall.

A confusion of light and lines blurred her vision as if she had stared at a candle flame for too long. "I didn't—"

"Shut up, swine. Soon Naabak's wife and armies will be mine. And you will be no more."

She clawed at his hands. The overwhelming need

to breathe roared in her chest. Yanking a finger from her throat, she rasped, "But...Naabak—"

Hot breath puffed in her face. She did not flinch. Her curse spared her the stench.

"Your Naabak battles fever from the day's ride. Demons torment his mind. Soon his stubs won't be able to wield a sword. Even if he lives, he will be useless to the king. And all that is his will pass to me." Konath's crazy-eyed squint sent a shiver across her skin. "Your last memory will be of me taking my pleasures before you die."

She held his stare, too terrified to look elsewhere. He eased the pressure on her neck, but kept her pinned to the wall. She hung in the air against the wall like one of Reumah's tapestries. Laughter barked in her flawed ears.

Konath released his fierce grip.

She fell to the floor and lay like a corpse until his footsteps faded into the night.

Rolling to her side, she cradled her ribs. Her bones ached like a paddled rug. She breathed thanks to God for restraining Konath. The vile man had not slaked his lust with her, or Reumah. But Naabak could not succumb to his disease. If God allowed Naabak to die, her end would be the same as the day of her capture.

"You fared better than me." Mereb bent to examine her body.

Hannah pushed him away. She did not have the strength to explain about her deformed ears and her curse this night.

"He did not draw blood. Must have been the wine he drank this evening."

Wine? Her mouth gaped. "You knew he was in there?" She scrambled to her feet. "And you sent me in?"

"Someone had to stop the adultery. I am of no consequence."

She shoved him toward the opening to her room. "Get. Out. You have sealed my tomb with your trickery."

Mereb grasped at her tunic. "You have found favor with Naabak. Your presence is a reminder to Reumah of their vows."

"And Naabak is dying." The force of her words pained her throat. "If Konath succeeds our master, all that belongs to Naabak—you, me, Reumah—will belong to that animal."

"So be forthright with Reumah. Speak to her of your time spent with her husband." Mereb touched her hand.

She drew back. "It is my first day. I have barely served her."

"You are both young," Mereb said, a hint of pleading in his voice. "Think of Naabak. He is not the one in the bed of another."

"Is he able?" Hannah's hand clapped over her mouth. She was the virgin daughter of a priest. To be discussing marital relations with a man was forbidden. "You must leave." She rubbed her bruised arm.

"Naabak spared my life and yours. He deserves our allegiance."

"Is there not a priest or elder in Aram that can heal him? I have heard of the temple sacrifices in Damascus. Certainly there is a medium in this heathen land?"

Mereb shook his head. "The king has inquired of his officials. They have tried spells and talked to spirits, but Naabak still suffers."

Hannah closed her eyes. She envisioned the boy

dancing before the prophet singing praises to Jehovah. Would the mouthpiece of God heal Naabak? Show him mercy because of his disease? With her enslavement, how could she speak to the man of God and tell him of the kindness Naabak had shown to a Hebrew captive? God did not take away her curse and she was the daughter of a chief priest.

She glanced out the window at the stars taking charge of the darkness. Longing filled her heart, for her homeland, for Gil. *Oh, Gilead. If only I had your bravery.*

"You must go to our mistress and remind her of her position." Mereb dropped to his knees. A trickle of sweat dripped from beneath his turban. "Reumah can keep us both safe from Konath."

She laughed at the insanity of her situation. At a Moabite bowing at her feet. At the hope that Konath could be restrained by another man's wife. Mereb did not join in her madness. He gave her a you-know-I-speak-the-truth stare. A stare she had seen in the eyes of her parents.

"Is Konath gone?" She studied Mereb's expression for the truth. She did not want to interrupt another lust-filled interlude.

He nodded. "To his men."

Befriending Reumah and gaining her trust was the only means of survival. If Hannah had any hope of returning to Jerusalem and seeing her family again, she had to return to the bedroom of iniquity and make amends.

9

Hannah paced outside the vine-swept doors of Reumah's bedroom. She would beg if need be and take the blame for barging into Reumah's bed chamber. Naabak had to be kept alive. Fever or no fever. If Konath came to power, Reumah's protection would cease. Konath would rule this household, take his sexual pleasure, and slit Hannah's throat. An ending he had vowed.

Did she dare mention the prophet of Israel to Reumah? Did Reumah wish for her husband's healing? Or was she waiting to warm Konath's bed? Oh, how Hannah longed to return to her own land.

With a deep breath, she knocked. The pain of Konath's beating radiated down her spine.

"Enter," came Reumah's reply.

Reumah reclined in the chair by the honey jar, lazily stirring the nectar. She didn't look up from the circles her finger created. "You will not judge me."

She knelt in front of her mistress, face to the floor. "What is there to judge? I am a lowly servant and I entered your chamber unannounced." *Because of Mereb's deception.*

"Hah. I saw your face." Reumah jolted forward in her seat. "Do not lie. You thought me shameful."

"You stunned me." Hannah tried not to cast blame. "I did not expect another man to be in your bed."

"He was not in my bed." Reumah pounded the table.

Hannah's muscles tensed at Reumah's harsh denial. By the letter of the law, he was not in her bed!

"You were not forthright earlier." Reumah ripped away Hannah's head covering. Cool air bathed Hannah's ear nubs. "Konath warned me about your cunning." Reumah pulled Hannah's hair as she drew back.

At the mention of Konath's name, Hannah's jaw clenched. Her hands fisted, embedding fingernails into her palms. He had tried to force himself on a virgin and now he soiled Naabak's bed. Did he give the order to murder Gil? Or did Konath slay Gil himself?

She stayed on her knees, but she would not stay silent. "Your husband knows of my curse. He spared my life and deemed me fit to serve his wife." She let her last word, the one of Reumah's position, linger in the air. "As you heard from his own lips, Konath knows as well. But he is not a man to trust with secrets." She braced for a slap. None came.

Reumah bent over as if in pain. She rested her elbows on her knees and wept into her hands. "I have failed. I have birthed no heir for Naabak. When he dies, his land and wealth will go to his father's people." Reumah's chest heaved as she swiped tears from her cheeks. "I will live in my family's home a bitter widow, handing bracelets to my brothers to sell in the marketplace for my keep." She swept another tear from her face and perfected her posture. "If Konath favors me, I will retain my wealth and position."

Hannah caressed her blood-stained knuckle, a gift

from Konath. Why should she care about the fate of this foreign woman? A heathen caught in adultery—with Konath no less. Gil protected the widows and downtrodden in the gleaning fields. Would he have taken pity on Reumah and championed her plight? She remembered Gil offering the pomegranate berries and coming to her defense when her brother's temper flared. Her heart ached. Gil would have helped Reumah find peace in her distress.

She bit her lip, fighting back the pain of losing Gil and her family. "I know of someone who could heal your husband." The words rushed from her mouth before she could censor them.

"Who?" Curiosity brightened Reumah's features.

"There is a prophet in Israel. I have seen him heal—"

Reumah rose and dismissed the announcement with a flip of her hand. "Naabak has seen officials at Hadad's temple."

"But has Naabak seen an official grow a leg?" She followed Reumah to the bed and did not picture what had passed on the sheets. "A lame boy danced before my eyes. Skin grew on bone. New flesh." She hesitantly touched Reumah's back. "I believe the prophet could restore Naabak."

Reumah whirled on her "Did you petition this prophet? What of your ears? I do not see proper flesh. If this prophet of yours is so great, why did he not heal you? You stood in his presence."

Heat flooded Hannah's limbs and cheeks. "He touched me but he said it was not my time."

"And what if it's not my husband's time?" Reumah clutched a pillow to her breast. "He should accept the ridicule of this Jew?"

Hannah's mouth fell open at Reumah's callous blasphemy. *Oh Lord, forgive this mockery.* Knees weak, she dropped to the floor before her mistress.

"It has to be Naabak's time." Her words rose with hope. "Naabak has no time to spare."

Reumah sprawled on the bed, her hair splaying across her headrest. Her gaze rested on the ceiling and danced from one rendering to another.

Hannah removed her mistress's sandals and sat by the bed.

"You have given me a thought. Naabak has seen the priests at the temple but not the king's advisor. He has the standing of a god. I shall ask the king to grant me a personal meeting with his priest. He knows Naabak is loyal to him. There is no greater power in all of Aram. If the king's priest hears what the God of Israel can do, he should be able to do more."

"It is not the same." Hannah jumped to her feet. "My eyes have seen a miracle of the Most High God."

"Israel does not house all the gods. I will send a swift chariot to the king's palace tomorrow." Reumah leaned forward. "You and Mereb be ready to accompany me to the house of Hadad when our letters arrive."

"I cannot attend you in the worship of another god." Her heart raced at the thought of breaking the Commandments of God. She gripped the bed to steady herself. "My father and brother are priests."

"You forget your place, slave." Reumah lunged across the bed and grasped Hannah's tunic. "We will go to the house of Hadad, and I will show you there are powerful gods in Aram. The king's priest can intercede for us and save my husband." Her grip loosened. "Now ready me for bed."

Hannah struggled to untie Reumah's sash. How could a daughter of a Levite priest step foot in a pagan temple? There was no sacrifice grand enough to wipe away this sin. She could hide this abomination from her family, but with the Hebrew God, there were no secrets.

But she was a slave now. How did a slave ignore the order of a master and keep her life? Especially when the master was Konath's mistress?

Panic seized her. She would be breaking God's first commandment not to worship any other gods. Would a jealous Jehovah overlook her entry into the House of Hadad? Tears wetted her eyes as if she walked through a windstorm in the wilderness.

A spited God did not heal curses.

10

Three days passed before letters from the king arrived. Three more days passed before Hannah and Reumah were rid of their flow. And she endured three face slaps for refusing to travel to Hadad's temple.

You shall have no other gods before me.

Commandment broken.

Remember the Sabbath day by keeping it holy.

Another commandment broken.

How many more coals could be heaped upon her head?

She clutched the side of a sleek war chariot and tried to stay on her sandaled feet. Mereb stood at her back, a fortress wall keeping her from fleeing. Reumah traveled alone. Her indigo and scarlet scarves fluttered faster than the stallion's mane.

Hannah pulled her head covering tight to preserve the elaborate braids Reumah insisted she wear to impress the pagan priest. She shielded her face from the windblown dirt, kicked up by speed of the horses while the rock strewn terrain jarred the cart of the chariot. The loose cut of her dress rippled against her body.

A hollow sensation filled her bones as the domed temple came into view. Her stomach churned like a violent sea. Damascenes leaned out of windows, curious to the pounding of hooves and wheels that normally whisked soldiers to battle.

Columns stood, one after the other, on both sides of the doors to Hadad's place of worship.

As the chariot slowed, she turned and clutched Mereb's robe. A fine layer of dust lightened the grooved scowl in his dark-raisin skin.

"I cannot do this." Her voice quaked with a holy fear.

"You must do as our master's wife says." Mereb gripped her wrists.

"*Which* master?"

"You will do what Reumah asks of you. Nothing less." He pulled her toward the back of the chariot. "Our mistress waits."

Official-looking men stood outside the temple, heads shaven, bodies dressed in finely woven tunics. Their arms and ankles glimmered with polished-bronze bands. Slow of stride, she and Mereb followed behind Reumah. The bald men clasped their hands together and smiled broadly as Reumah sauntered toward the entrance to the temple.

"What will my duty be?" she whispered to Mereb while the officials greeted Reumah. "You must have accompanied Reumah here before."

"Do not worry. You will be shown what to do." Mereb hooked his arm through hers as they entered a dim foyer. An official's gaze dropped lower and lower as he inspected the drape of her gown. His seductive stare slithered across her skin.

She slowed her steps and adjusted to the lack of light in the large room. In the distance, lamps burned in a semi-circle around a statue she assumed was Hadad. The Aramean idol had eyes sculpted like flaming suns and a gaping mouth, which seemed to mock her.

They walked on a stone bridge, over a sunken arena, and toward the false god. Something moved below the bridge. A haze of incense smoke clouded the room, making it difficult to see what lay below.

She squinted into the depths. "Are those snakes?" she asked Mereb.

Mereb's chuckle blended into the faint chants and moans that filled the arena. "You would think of animals with your Hebrew sacrifices. Those are people. Worshipping with their bodies."

"Together?" Her mouth gaped open.

More Moabite laughter.

She coughed from the smoke, or shock, or both. "But we are not...I mean...Reumah is not here to have relations?"

No answer.

She hesitated. Would Hadad's priest lie with a foreigner? Her ears buzzed with the gasps from the shadows.

Mereb tightened his grip on her arm.

They followed Reumah through a door and entered a private, candlelit chamber.

Blinking, she welcomed the brightness of the room. An older priest sat on a golden throne, fully clothed in an embroidered robe and flanked by an ornately dressed elder. Releasing a pent-up breath, she mumbled a prayer and embraced the calm like a cool trade wind. At least she wasn't in that wanton arena.

"Holy one." Reumah bowed before the priest. Her voice was reverent but unsteady.

Hannah locked her knees in protest. How could she bow to this man? *You shall have no other gods.*

Mereb yanked her down to the floor. Her arm

went numb. *Forgive me, Lord.*

The priest reached out to Reumah. "I have heard of your need. If your offering is acceptable, I will intercede with Hadad on the king's authority. Your husband will be spared."

The priest stood.

The robe fell.

Hannah gasped. All she saw was flesh and gold. Gold bracelets on the man's arms. Gold piercings through his nipples. A gold ring through his navel. She scanned no further.

The man looked from Reumah to…her. "She is a virgin?"

Reumah nodded.

No, no, no!

He stretched his gold-ringed hand toward her.

A shiver streaked through her veins. The walls swayed—leaning left, spinning right. This was not what her father and brothers practiced in the temple.

Hannah scrambled to her feet.

Mereb fisted a clump of her skirt.

She kicked at his chest. "You told me not to worry."

"I lied."

11

Hadad's priest snapped his fingers at Mereb. "Bring her to me."

Hannah desired to see Naabak healed but not in this manner. She would not lay with this pagan priest, a priest with no power to restore Naabak. Touching his nakedness was unthinkable, unclean, an abomination to her God.

She punched at Mereb's treasonous arms. A holy rage wracked her body. She would not betray her heritage, her father, the line of Zebula. "*Shalom.* Please. Let me go." Her plea echoed in her ears.

Reumah rose from her knees. "Servant, bow low and do as the advisor says. You are in Hadad's chambers."

"I beg of you," she rasped, her throat tight and dry like a nomad's rope. "You do not want me. I am cursed." She ripped off her head covering. "See." She lifted the hair from her ears. "I am crippled. Unworthy." *Lord, have this curse be good for something.*

"Now," Reumah demanded.

Mereb circled her waist with his arm. His rough hand cupped her mouth. Or was it the elder's? She did not know. Time moved too fast.

"Liar." Hannah's words vibrated against the fleshy palm of her vile captor. She struggled to get free. With no weapons within her reach, she attacked with her fingernails. She clawed at any arm, any face, any strip of bare flesh.

"Is she possessed?" The priest raised his arm to strike her.

Reumah laughed as if the priest's comment was a compliment from a younger lover. "A frightened virgin is all, my Lord."

Hannah bucked her head to dislodge Mereb's hand from her lips. "Yes. Posse—"

Mereb's palm flattened her tongue.

Reumah stomped her foot and chastised her servants.

Mereb cinched Hannah's waist and lifted her feet from the floor. "You will submit for Naabak."

She would not submit for Naabak or anyone. Flinging her head back into the Moabite's nose, she used his tight grip on her waist as leverage to kick her feet. His thumb slipped back into her throat. She bit down and gagged.

A wave of pressure rose from her stomach. Her throat sizzled. Vomit filled her mouth. Mereb tried to dam its outpouring. She couldn't breathe.

Her body tensed. She would not die here. Not in a foreign land. Not in a foreign temple. She had to get air. She had to move Mereb's hand from her mouth. She had to, for God, for Gil, for—

She catapulted her fist into her fellow servant's eye.

Mereb stumbled backward.

Bile splattered from her mouth. Brown and yellow chunks covered the false priest's nakedness. Would this insult mean death?

The priest leapt from his chair. Reumah jumped backward. Bits of food clung to the hem of her gown.

"The spirits are attacking her." The priest swung incense in her direction. "Remove her."

Two bald elders flanked Hannah's sides. "To where?"

"Anywhere but here." The priest thrust his arm at the door in dismissal.

Praise be to the One True God. You have spared me a vulgar humiliation. Now spare me my master's wrath.

As they shoved her from the chamber, Reumah fell at the advisor's feet.

Hannah cleared her throat and ignored the searing pain in the center of her chest. She would show no weakness to these heathen guards. She would save her strength and forge a way back to her homeland. The land promised to her people.

Mereb followed in her wake. The bridge seemed longer now that they were leaving. He clutched his bruised eye and muttered hissing curses she did not understand.

Outside the temple, the afternoon sun commanded the sky. It had not changed since they entered the devil's den. She almost had. She almost lost her virginity to a vile Hadad worshipper. The crawl of beetle's legs shivered across her skin.

The chariots waited under the fronds of a fig tree. As they neared their cart, Mereb rounded on her. "How dare you attack me? Are you so lofty, Jew, that an Aramean man is beneath you?"

She clenched her molars to keep from spitting at him. The breeze could not cool the heat raging through her body. "Is that the task you were given? To get me beneath him? You wrestled me like livestock! Is it feeding time? Or are you like the priest needing pleasure?"

The whack of his hand rung in her ears. Her lip moistened. She touched it. Blood stained her fingers.

"We are here on Naabak's behalf. On your urging." Mereb boarded the chariot.

"My urging was to see the prophet in Israel. In Mahanaim. Not Damascus." Her accusation prompted a glare from the chariot driver.

"Where is the commander's wife?" The driver looked to Mereb for an answer, but his gaze inspected the stains on her garment.

Mereb leaned against the side of the cart. "Delayed. We are to return without our mistress."

She climbed into the chariot and stood behind Mereb.

"You are a perverse and wicked man. Your mouth spills forth lies." She kept her voice low and definite. "You have sent me into danger twice, but no more."

Mereb turned, cocked his chin, and peered down his nose. "What does a woman know of danger? Tell me after our mistress calls for you."

She slumped against the metal wall of the chariot. Should she have remained silent about the prophet of Israel? No. She spoke the truth. She owed a debt to Naabak for his kindness. But she would not wait for another bone-jarring beating. Tonight, she would be slave to Reumah's hand. But soon, too soon, it would be Konath's vengeful hand. And worse, his vile body.

Her bones would not disintegrate in Damascus. She would not allow it.

Escaping to Mahanaim was her only chance at seeing the prophet. He had to heal her this time so she could return home and ask forgiveness of her parents. That is what she and Gil had set out to do. She would finish their journey.

The chariot slowed as it neared the outskirts of Naabak's camp. The driver veered the horses toward the cliffs, toward a harvest-moon-shaped wall that joined a mountain. Six feet of vertical stone gave shade to the chariot and relief to her uncovered head.

"Why are we stopping?" Mereb asked. "We serve at the house."

She remembered what Reumah had told her that first day about leaving the house. Had Reumah withdrawn her protection because of the scene at the temple? Was this stop meant for revenge? Hannah shuddered at the thought of being left to fend off a group of men. She eyed the arena, the rows of seats, the driver.

The driver secured the reins.

She started as a loud clank sounded from within the stone walls. *Clank. Clink. Clank.* The clash of metal on metal rose from within the stone barrier. A battle of swords?

Mereb touched the soldier's shoulder. "Why the delay?"

The driver brushed by Mereb. "I go to see if it is still Naabak you serve."

"Naabak is here? Not in a tent?" Hope rose within her. The commander had saved her from punishment once before. Would he spare her again?

The driver jumped from the cart. "In his condition, he requires the coolness of the caves." The driver consulted two soldiers standing guard under an archway bearing the image of their fiery-eyed, false god. The three men strolled into the arena.

Laughter, deep and taunting, drifted out over the stone walls.

She stilled.

And listened.

To familiar words. Hebrew words. Words of judgment. The jeers reminded her of Gil's teasing tone when he mimicked his mother's call.

Can it be? Her body became light as air. Her heart pounded hard and fast like a celebratory drum, sending a ripple down her back as if a palm frond fanned her flesh.

Tank. Tank. Clink. Curses roared out. The praise of her God echoed over the wall.

She soared out of the chariot.

"Where are you going?" Mereb's words slurred together as if he was stunned by her initiative. "I will not risk rebuke coming to your defense."

"I am not asking you to." She charged toward the entrance to the ring. Her nerves sizzled like a frog landing on hot rocks.

Mereb trailed after her. "You fool. Come back in the cart. You will not get far."

She whirled around. Tears of joy welled in her eyes. "Go back to your perch. This does not concern you."

Mereb squinted in her direction. "That is Hebrew I hear. Do you know someone fighting in that arena?" Mereb crossed his arms and made a questioning humming sound.

She left him planted halfway between the chariot and the enclosure. Peering into the arena, she searched for the voice. Please let it be him.

A soldier pointed a sword at the back of a man clad in a loin cloth. The man had no tunic to absorb the blood streaking down his left arm. The pair walked toward the mountain to a gated entrance. Before they entered, the injured man scuffled with one of the guards. The first soldier seized the man's arms, twisting the bloody gash. She cringed at the pain he must have endured.

The wounded man shouted curses at the soldier.

She knew that defiant stance.

His head swiveled her direction.

She knew that defiant grin.

Blood pounded from her temples to her toes. Praise leapt from her lips.

My Gil is alive.

But for how long?

12

The delight in finding Gil alive was a bitter root. The Aramean soldiers had not slain Gil in the village, but by the looks of his bloodied body, they would cast him off soon enough. Gil's place was in the fields outside of Jerusalem, not in a fortress outside of Damascus.

Her throat tightened. She would not leave Gil to die alone in a mountain. His life would not end in anguish.

She called to Mereb. "Where does that opening in the mountain go?"

Mereb eyed her as though she had asked for the King's secrets. "There are caves in the mountain. Captives are held in them. It is of no concern of yours, or is it?"

She rushed into the arena, tripped, and fell in the dirt, her thoughts and plans outpacing her feet. She had to go to Gil. He'd protected her. She could not abandon him to a slow death. Not at the hands of these barbarians.

"Oh Adonai, give me wisdom," she mumbled as she rose.

"Have you been in the heat too long?" Mereb grabbed hold of her sleeve. She swatted at his hand. "Those caves are dark. The souls of the men inside are darker still. They will ravish an innocent like you. And woe to the woman who does not die swiftly."

She marched ahead. She was not afraid of dying. How often had Gil faced death in the arena? Every day?

"If you enter the mountain, it is almost certain you will not come out. You think yourself too good for the priest, but you will give yourself to a host of brutes?" Mereb chastised her as though she were a wayward child. "Reumah will hold me accountable for your rebellion. No one is worth this calamity."

"Yes, someone is." She licked her lips. Her tongue had little moisture to share. "If Naabak is in the caves, he will help me." Her hope became her prayer.

"It is not for certain Naabak is inside. Or that he would favor your request." He held out his hand to her. "Come back to the chariot. Do not upset Reumah any more than you already have."

She met Mereb's authoritative gaze. Guilt and longing and shame pulsed behind her eyes, into her temples. *Gil suffers because of me. Lowly, sinful me.*

"You are returning to the house?" Mereb nodded as if she had already agreed to his wishes.

"I am going into the caves." She continued her journey through the arena, toward the mountain. She had one purpose, and one purpose only, to rescue Gil. She willed her hands to stop trembling. *Hear O' Israel, the Lord is our God.*

As she neared the mountain, the gate opened.

She halted and clasped her hands behind her, feigning an assignment.

The chariot driver stood in the doorway, hands on his hips.

"Charges obey or they are beaten until they do." The driver reached for her arm.

She stepped backward. "And what of the charge given us?" She indicated a far-off Mereb, statue still. "Our mistress desired we console her husband and bring word of his health." Her indignation rose to the heavens. "You ran off before we could inquire of you." The louder she spoke, the bolder she became.

The driver snorted a laugh. "No one sees Naabak except for our new commander. Konath is protected from the plague by the gods."

Were these the same gods that protected Naabak? Konath seemed sure of his immortality.

Mereb arrived at her side, catching his breath from an apparent hurried stroll.

She shot the Moabite a crinkled-nose glare. Was he going to help her see Naabak after all, or was this another scheme like his trickery in the temple?

"Naabak is the commander until his death...or until removal by the King...not Konath." Mereb spoke between breaths. "To speak otherwise is punishable by death."

"How dare you question me?" The driver grabbed Mereb's cloak. "You are nothing but dung for the fire."

"You speak the truth." She placed a protective hand on Mereb's shoulder, unwilling to see Mereb bloodied like Gil. He may be of some help to her with his knowledge of the caves. "Our lives are worth far less than the lives of the King's soldiers. That is why we were sent to seek out Naabak. If we perish, others will come to take our place." Her declaration seemed to calm the soldier's rage. Bowing with her face to the ground, she added hastily, "Great are you defender of Aram."

She glanced up at their driver. It took memories of Gil's beating to flood her eyes with tears of sincerity.

"May I ask for your protection inside the mountain? We began this journey under your authority."

The soldier released Mereb, but she remained low, beseeching him from the dirt.

Mereb knelt beside her. His lips moved but no sound came forth.

The soldier scanned the area. "Get up." He shoved Mereb toward the opening. Her forced humility and flattery had worked.

Leaving the afternoon sun behind, she stepped into the shadows of a large mountain tomb filled with rock and shadows and tunnels. The tunnels wound to the right and left of the opening. Torches cast a halo of light but left a trail of soot on the rock. She touched the wall to steady herself and shuddered from the cool stone. *Oh God, I do not need to slay thousands as King David. I need to save one man, one of your servants.*

Mereb and the driver turned to the east. She followed. They headed toward a planked door with an armed guard.

The scuff of sandals echoed in the corridor. Was it Naabak? Had he been told of visitors?

Up ahead, men emerged from a bend in the passageway. Her heart seized, beating like a frightened dove's wings. Konath and two soldiers blocked their path. She recognized one of the men. He had mocked Gil.

"My Lord," the driver said, clearing room for Konath to pass. "Naabak's wife has sent her servants to aid her husband."

Hannah glanced back the way they had come. Could she race to the light without getting caught? To the chariot? And what then?

Konath's breath warmed the top of her head. His

hand brushed her cheek while his grip on her arm stopped the rush of blood.

"You could not stay away from me?" His chuckle hollowed her stomach.

An answer gurgled in her throat. "We came to—"

"Seduce me? Or satisfy my men?" Konath backed her against the stone wall. Juts in the rock pricked her skin. Her thin dress did little to stop the pain.

"Naabak gave me to his wife," she said, hoping the name of the king's commander would spare her ruin.

"She is not here." The rumble in his voice raised the hairs on her skin like a swarm of locusts had come to feed on her flesh. "And my captives thirst for a woman."

"No," she screamed, pushing his chest in earnest to dislodge her prey. "Leave me be. What you do to me, you do to Reumah."

"Wait," Mereb said.

She stilled, but her muscles tensed, ready for a fight. Thankfully, soldiers bore witness to this injustice. Naabak had saved her from his second-in-command before. Surely, Konath saw the peril in harming the commander's gift to his wife.

Mereb pointed toward the arena. "I believe she seeks a man. A Hebrew. One who recently fought outside."

"He lies!" Traitor! "I seek Naabak. No other." The force of her denial burned her throat. Jerking her arm, she squirmed to get free.

Konath held fast and lifted her closer to his foul mouth. "What sport to see a Hebrew dog fight to save his bitch." Konath's cackle made her soul tremble.

She dropped her weight to the ground and kicked

in a frenzy. Flailing her right arm, she lashed out at anything in the path of her fist. Her hand met bronze-embedded leather. Her knuckles throbbed and her fingers numbed. She needed Naabak. Where was he?

Breath surged from her lungs. "Naa—"

Konath's hand muffled her scream. He dragged her toward the planked door.

"Open it," Konath demanded of the guards.

Air rushed from her nostrils. She continued to summon Naabak. His name reverberated in Konath's palm. Clawing at the ground with her feet, her curled toes bent the leather of her sandals.

Metal scraped on metal as the latch lifted and the door opened.

Konath shoved her into the dark cave, face first.

"Mereb. Please." Her scream rang out as she skidded on her chest in a slop of mud.

She scrambled to her feet. Her body tensed, ready for what lay in wait for her in the shadows.

The glow from the torch in the tunnel revealed bodies. Men's bodies. Moving toward her.

"I will see you after," Konath jeered. "One riot is enough for today."

The door slammed shut, leaving her in darkness. Muffled congratulatory laughter rumbled on the other side of the planks.

In a breath, hands ripped at her clothes like vultures tugging on raw meat. She punched and pounded and bit.

"Gil," she rasped, frantic for his answer. "*Shalom.* Merciful God."

"Hannah?"

His voice was like an angel's trumpet. "Gil. I am here."

He cursed, loud and guttural. The would-be rapists were cast aside like rags. A protective arm encircled her waist.

"You uncircumcised pagans. Unhand my wife."

13

She hid behind Gil, the man who had declared to the barbarians that he was her husband. Could it be that their bond still held even though Gil suffered in this pagan pit on her account?

Shouts, some of them Hebrew, some of them foreign, erupted from the darkness. Backing into a wall, she ravaged anything that reached around Gil's protective shield. Flesh pounded on flesh. Bodies fell. Groans rose from the floor. Panic seized her muscles. Her arms trembled from the tension.

Squinting into the darkness, her eyes sought Gil. How long could he last? Against how many men? She remembered his bloodied arm from the arena and lashed out at any brush of her clothing. It was not much help, but it was some.

"Benjamin. Stand for me," Gil called to another in Hebrew. The intensity of his request sent shivers dancing over her exposed skin.

A careful arm embraced her shoulders. Gil enfolded her into his chest. It was slick. She hoped not with blood.

"Come. Now." Gil pulled her from the fight, leaving the crazed men to devour each other.

Gil led her through the darkness. How could he navigate without light? It was not impossible, but with every step she feared tumbling or striking stone. A sea of harsh rocks pierced the soles of her bared feet. She ignored the pain, relishing the distance from the other captives.

She jerked sideways. Gil lifted her off the ground and set her in an alcove. Damp stone guarded her back. Gil guarded her front. She was safely wedged in a recess with a man she feared had been murdered because he fought for her.

Gil's breath tickled the side of her face. "I prayed you were safe. Now you share my pit."

"Will they not follow?" She pressed her cheek against his. She wanted to feel the rumble of his words. The bristle of his beard. The hammering of his heart.

"Benjamin is tall and strong." She could almost hear a grin in his voice. "There are only three others and one is injured." Three? It seemed they had fought a legion.

She collapsed into his chest. His embrace joined their bodies. She reached up and stroked his jaw. He held her fingers on his face. There would be no chastisement for their closeness. Gil was alive. God had answered one prayer.

"I thought you were dead," she whispered through ragged breaths. "I looked for you on the journey…" Tears slowed her words.

"I was bound and gagged like a criminal. They slung me over an ass and left me with the herds." His voice was hushed, but she could hear the anger low in his throat.

"When I saw you today. With the soldiers. I could not leave you to die. Not again." She quieted her sobs and nestled into his neck. "We should have stayed in Jerusalem."

He shook his head. "I wanted to come on this

journey. Whatever happens, remember that." His hands slid into her hair and stilled over her ear nubs. His jaw tensed. "What have they done to you?" Fury hovered in his hushed voice.

She withdrew her hands from his face and tried to pull his fingers from her deformed skin. "Nothing. They have done nothing. I have been this way since birth." She hesitated and held her breath, anticipating that he would pull away. Abandon her to the other prisoners. But he remained close.

She clasped his hand in hers and held it over her heart. *Do not pull away for me.* "It is another curse."

"Why didn't you tell me?" He brushed the hair from her nub. "You told me about the other curses. Did you not trust me with this?"

The hurt in his question caused new tears to flood her cheeks. She closed her eyes for she had not been forthright.

She was glad she could not see his expression clearly, or he, hers. She slumped against her stone backrest. "You cannot see the others. But my deformity is ugly. I am ugly. For look where I have brought us."

"You did not bring us here. Those heathens did." He rested a hand on her shoulder. "I wanted to be with you. I still do." His thumb outlined her lip. "Now. And afterward. If God is willing."

Breath hitched in her chest. Was there even a chance at an afterward? Did he believe they would escape from this prison? That she would be healed? That her betrothal to Azor would be forgotten? Oh, if it could be so. But she was not whole. Her vessel was still stained. How far had the chief priest's daughter fallen that she wore vomit-stained rags in a pit full of lustful pagans.

"God is deaf when it comes to my prayers. But he should not forsake you and Benjamin on my behalf." She reached for Gil's arm. He winced. "Oh, Gil, you suffer and bleed. Forgive me. Please, forgive me."

"It is not you I have to forgive. The kings of Israel and Aram signed for peace. Were we not on our land? Seeking our prophet?"

"Because I am cursed." She burrowed her face into the curve of his neck. "One day I hope to learn of my ancestor's offense and why God chose to punish me." Her voice faltered. "I do not want you punished because of my transgressions."

"I am not afraid of a fight. I have grown up fighting. It is but a sport to me." His voice rose as if he remembered sparring in Jerusalem's alleys.

"Back. Back," rang out in the cave. Echoes of Hebrew came first. Then Aramaic.

A tremor shot through her body. She desired to be strong for Gil, but her strength grew weary.

"Benjamin is one with us," Gilead assured her. The weight of his chin rested on her head.

"I do not want to perish at Konath's hand. He is a wicked man."

Gil's body stiffened. "Has he hurt you?"

"No," fled from her mouth. She didn't want Gil thinking she had been defiled. "Naabak offered me protection. I serve his wife. If I had refused his offer, I would have served Konath. And I would have begged to die by the flash of a sword."

Gilead's hands slipped between her back and the stone wall. "God spared you."

"For a season. But Naabak lies dying of the plague. When he is taken from this life, I will belong to Konath."

"Never. It will not be." Gil's tone held the fight of a caged animal.

Her fingers wove into his hair. His thick curls were like tendrils coiling around her skin. His breaths fell atop of hers. His lips hovered at the side of her mouth. When he whispered her name, she wished he had spoken it between her lips.

Heat flushed up her neck and into her cheeks. The pump, pump, pump of her heart radiated out over her limbs like a storm waking the Dead Sea. How cruel to have such yearning for a man and not be bound to him.

"Gil," she whispered, "We may have no other time than this moment. I am willing to begin an afterward." She turned so her lips were a hair width above his.

His lips descended upon hers. His desire consumed her. A geyser of pleasure burst within her belly. *Oh God, Do not take him from me.*

Noise interrupted their kiss. Rebukes.

"Where is that Hebrew?" A man bellowed.

Flickering light split the darkness.

Gil turned and wedged her into the nook with his body. They were trapped. His bravery was useless.

"Hannah?" Reumah's summons was like a luxurious soak in eucalyptus oil. "Mereb insisted she was in here. Where is my servant?"

A torch flame bathed Hannah and Gil in light. The fire bearer unsheathed his sword. "She is here," he announced.

Two soldiers tore Gil from her. He thrashed in defiance.

She gasped at the blood and dirt covering his body. The darkness had been kind to spare her his plight.

"I dream of spilling your blood," a soldier said, scratching at Gil's dried wounds.

"Stop," Hannah shouted for all of Damascus to hear. "Let him be." She stepped closer to the light bearer. "If you touch him, I will awaken your gods with my screams."

"What if I touch you?" The torch flickered in her direction. A wicked grin crossed his face.

"Mistress! I am here. Save us."

The flames moved closer to Gil's curly hair.

"Bring her to me." The tremble in Reumah's voice hinted her patience had waned. "She was a gift from my husband."

She stretched to her full height and glared at the guards as if she were Naabak's daughter. Pointing at Gil, she said, "I will not leave here without him." She would not abandon Gil in this filthy cave.

The soldiers squabbled in Aramean before pushing her toward Gil. Sheathed swords prodded their backs as they made their way to the entrance. Captives lined the entryway where Konath had thrust her to her ruin. Her brow furrowed at the men who had attempted to remove her clothing.

She stopped in front of a young man. A man she remembered from the village running to save his sheep. This must be Benjamin. Bruises darkened the side of Benjamin's face. She owed him a debt. Benjamin's strength and bravery had given her and Gil time to hide and be together. He had suffered abuse on her behalf. Her soul ached at his battered body.

"*Toda raba*, Benjamin," she whispered.

His eyes shone through the shadows. "Are we not one people?"

"Always," she said, glancing at Gil.

When Hannah crossed the threshold, Reumah backed away, fanning her nose.

"Hah," Konath snorted. "This is what your husband gifts you? A whore in soiled rags?"

Gil spat on the floor. "Do you not fear God? Or your commander?" His reprimand hung in the corridor.

The *whaa-aack* of a whip split Gil's shoulder.

Hannah screamed and lurched forward to shield Gil from another attack.

A soldier seized her arms.

Gil folded in pain, but guards held him upright.

Blood seeped from the lash. She struggled against the soldier's strong hold. His restraint kept her from comforting Gil.

"Next time leave the punishment to me." Konath unhanded the whip from his soldier. "Take him to the arena."

No! Gil did not deserve to die. Her body tensed. "Reumah," she called using her private address, "I beg of you. Bring him to the house."

The soldier escorting Gil hesitated.

"Take him outside," Konath roared. His cheeks turned a deep shade of plum. "He is of no use to the lady."

"Spare him, Mistress." Her gaze did not leave Reumah's face. "Has your sacrifice at the temple pleased Hadad? Has he acted on your behalf?"

Reumah waved Hannah's soldier off and stepped away from Konath. Gil disappeared down the tunnel.

"In time. The gods will act." Reumah fingered the loop of her gold earring.

"Are your gods asleep?" Hannah accentuated her last word. Her gaze darted to Konath.

Konath petted his sword.

"Is your god any better?" Reumah spat her last word in Hannah's face.

Hannah tilted her head and pretended to be the mistress while Reumah played the offending servant. "You will never know," Hannah said in the voice of a noble. "And neither will Naabak."

Reumah jerked away at the mention of her husband's name. She licked her lips over and over as her eyes blinked a code.

"Wait," Reumah called out. "I could use a strong servant."

"So you want me to make the dog a eunuch?" Konath laughed as if he preferred this request. He lowered his piercing eyes until they were even with Reumah's. "You are the commander's wife. We shall make the Hebrew fit to suit you."

Was there no end to this wickedness? Heat engulfed her neck and burned hotter than a stoked furnace. Flashes of light blurred her vision as her bones became like piles of ash. She turned toward Reumah, tears streaming down her cheeks, into her mouth. "He is my husband." A righteous lie.

A calloused hand smothered her mouth. But flesh could not stop her plea. Her voice continued to squeak and beckon.

"My head splits with all this turmoil," Reumah stuttered, "I need rest."

"The woman does not know what she wants," Konath said, dismissing Reumah with a flip of his hand. His yellow-toothed grin fell on Hannah. "Kill the boy. Let the birds have a feast."

Hatred roared inside Hannah's soul. Hatred for Aram, for Konath, for her own God. A God who had abandoned her at birth. Gilead was faithful to the Law. He did not deserve to be skewered like a rabbit on a spit.

She whirled on the torch bearer and struck his arm. Cinders flew into the air. Reumah screamed.

Hannah ran. Not toward the light of the arena, but into the shadows of the tunnel. She raced deeper into the mountain, around the bend that Konath had appeared from. Her lips pleaded, over and over, for Naabak.

Every breath she took beckoned the commander. "Please. Naabak. Answer me."

She would follow the line of torches to the borders of Aram if need be. Her eyes flooded with tears of mourning. Gil had to stay alive. Naabak's name screeched from her mouth. The sound, sharp like a blade on a silversmith's wheel, threatened to unearth the rocks around her.

Heavy footfalls followed her. The thunder grew louder. A tug on her tunic foiled her flight.

She slid in the pebbled dirt.

"Naabak. Help," she screeched. The fire in her chest made her lungs feel like roasted dates. A soldier up ahead blocked her path.

A triumphant cackle blared behind her. Something grazed the flap of her ear nub. "Hah!"

Her shoulder collapsed in pain. She slumped to the ground. The *thunk* of a wooden club narrowly missed her hip. She cried out for Naabak.

Konath cursed. His weapon was at the ready to pulverize her bones.

"Israel?" The voice came from a room up ahead.

Konath stilled and looked toward the guard.

Everyone had heard the summons. It was weak,

yet somehow powerful.

"Naabak, I am here." She struggled to her feet, clutching her collar bone.

The guard stepped away.

"Bring her," came the order.

She didn't wait to be brought. She sprinted toward her salvation.

14

Hannah rushed through the rounded opening in the mountain's inner wall. The soldier standing guard did not follow. He skidded short of entering Naabak's infectious tomb. A flickering lamp illuminated the cave and what looked to be a partially decayed corpse.

"Master?" Hannah gasped. Her rescuer had little hair, no ears, no lips, few teeth. Only rotting wounds covered his once-rugged face.

Dropping to her knees beside a raised bed, she whispered, "Oh, Master. What has become of you?"

Naabak struggled to speak. Coughing and sputtering he choked on his spit.

She quickly grabbed a cloth from a water basin and dabbed at Naabak's face, moistening his raw, festering skin. Heat radiated from his scalp.

"You are with fever." She hesitated to touch his forehead, but she needed this man alive. "I can help you." She did not look away from the swollen slits of his eyes, but beheld his deformity with the reverence of a daughter. "But I need you to help me in this moment as well. You must save a Hebrew slave for me. My beloved. My Gilead." Her plea stuttered from her parched throat.

Naabak raised a stump of a hand and tried to motion her away from the bed.

He was kindhearted to think of her health but all

she could think about was Gil and the beating he suffered at the hand of Konath and his men. Her body shook.

Her arms trembled as she placed a cloth on Naabak's forehead. "Do not save me. Save my Gilead. I beg of you."

A raspy "Who?" came from the opening that once was Naabak's mouth.

"Her husband." Reumah answered from the doorway, a veil covering her nose. Tears streaked her alabaster-powdered cheeks.

She met Reumah's gaze. Naabak's wife had saved her once this day. Would she show mercy again or remember the scene at the temple?

"He is her lover." Konath stood behind Reumah in the tunnel. Neither came near Naabak.

She would not allow a corrupt heathen to tarnish Gil's name or cast her as a harlot.

"Gil accompanied me to see our prophet." Her throat swelled as she remembered what Gil had suffered by escorting her on this journey. She sat tall on her knees so Naabak could see her earnestness. "Do not let him die for his kindness to me. For I know you can be kind and just as well."

Naabak struggled to sit up. Fresh blood stained the sheet where his hands lay. His breathy groans filled the room. "Bring me the Jew." Naabak's command sounded like a determined whisper. He raised his arm toward the guard in the doorway.

The soldier did not move.

"Did you not hear?" Reumah shrieked, her eyes wide with indignation. "Your commander has spoken. Bring him the slave from above."

Konath brushed by Reumah and gripped the

soldier's shoulder. "My Lord, the slave is as good as dead by now. This girl has troubled you for nothing. She does not know her place."

"If the Hebrew has survived this long, he has skill. Make haste. The men will listen to my second." Naabak's eyes closed.

The guard bowed toward Naabak and hurried off to carry out the order.

Hannah leaned over Naabak's shriveled form. "How can I ever repay you?'

Naabak's eyes fluttered open. No sound came from his sore-laden mouth.

The scrunch of pebbles filtered into the cavern. Konath lingered in the tunnel. He hissed words at Reumah, but he saved his best just-wait leer for Hannah.

She turned, faced the ground, and prayed aloud. She would have sworn a spider crawled down her side.

When Konath was out of view, she slumped against Naabak's bed. Her bones were as paste. It took all her fortitude to stand and offer her gratitude to Reumah.

"I am doubly in your debt," she said, standing close enough for Reumah to hear her thankfulness, but not close enough to spread the disease. "You spared me humiliation in that pit. And now you champion for Gil's life."

Reumah stepped backward and briefly removed the veil from her nose. "Do not thank me for what has yet to be done. I do not know how much fight is left in your husband."

Tears pooled in Reumah's eyes. Hannah wondered if the woman truly spoke of Gil, or if the guilt of leaving Naabak to suffer alone while she committed adultery weighed on Reumah's soul.

"The stench is too much," Reumah sobbed.

Distant curses ricocheted off the tunnel walls.

If there was a time to beseech Reumah about the prophet, it was now. Hannah licked her lips and dredged up compassion for this woman with whom she had shared fellowship.

"Where is Hadad's miracle? Did the advisor not speak to the gods on your behalf?" She spoke as if to a weeping child. "Come to Israel. I will lead you. If Naabak is healed, your status does not change. You remain a wealthy woman with armies at your feet. If he dies, what will become of you?"

The linen fell from Reumah's face. "I have a home—"

"Has Konath sworn an oath to you?" She lowered her voice to barely a whisper as if she spoke a confidence. "Does he comfort you every night?"

A flash of doubt stilled Reumah's expression. "Konath is a man of position." Reumah smoothed the folds of her gown. "He is not always in camp."

Was Reumah blind to what awaited her? Did she truly trust Konath with her future? Hannah had to show Reumah that she may not end up a wife, but a concubine. "Does your king not have daughters of marrying age?"

"Stop it." Reumah shuddered and hugged her chest. The smell did not seem to be as rotten as the thought of her widowhood.

Hannah continued, "Bring me vessels of fresh water, hyssop, and cedar wood. Bandages and clean clothes. Your husband will be well enough to travel in a few days. The God of Israel will succeed where

Hadad fails. His prophet resides in Mahanaim, but for how long I do not know."

Konath's return interrupted her plea.

"You want this circumcised fool?" Konath shoved Gil into the small room. Gil stumbled and sank to his knees. Blood and bruises covered his body.

Cramps seized her stomach. How dare they whip Gil like a stubborn ox? Ignoring the pulsing pain in her belly, she rushed to Gil's aid.

"You should not be near the fever." She shifted Gil toward the wall for support. His armpits were the only part of his upper body not lashed and raw.

Konath chuckled. No remorse showed on his face. "You have lost a servant for the night." He guided Reumah down the hall. "I will not allow such freedoms with my slaves."

Hannah followed them to the threshold. "Please. Clean water and hyssop." Her voice echoed in the corridor. She didn't care if the soldiers heard and thought her brash, she would fight for Naabak's survival. "Tunics and strips of cloth."

Reumah hesitated. Her gaze fell to her feet. Had she caught her sandal on a rock or did she stumble from the shame of abandoning her husband in a burial chamber?

Reumah returned to the entrance of the catacomb.

Konath inspected his knuckle as if a scratch was more important than his intended bride.

"My lot is cast," Reumah said. "Leprosy has destroyed my husband and my future."

"Let me take you to the Holy Land." Hannah took a small step toward Reumah. "All things will be made new." The thrust of her last word was aimed at Reumah's conscience.

Naabak coughed.

Reumah's eyes glistened. "Not for me."

Konath called out in Aramean.

"Trust in the One True God," Hannah shouted. "You have to trust."

The guard stared at her as she beheld an empty tunnel.

A gurgling noise came from the bed.

She hurried to Naabak and patted a sponge to his disintegrated mouth. "Master," she whispered. "Seek the prophet in Israel. He can restore your body. I have seen flesh grow. New flesh. Right before my eyes." She swatted at the gnats wanting to nest on Naabak's face and wondered where she and Gil would finish their days. In the arena? In the pit? Or worse, she in Konath's bed while Gil rotted in a grave.

She picked up Naabak's nearly empty pitcher and poured a few drops of water in Gil's mouth. He brushed her arm like she had given him a feast.

"She is a daughter of Aaron, the brother of Moses." Gil's voice was uncharacteristically flat. No amusement rang in his words. "Her father atones for Israel's sins. It is the priest's duty to inspect skin for disease. Leprosy knows no borders between Aram and Israel." Gil closed his eyes. His declaration had worn on him like another beating.

"I know of what my father and brothers recite," she said, returning to Naabak's side. "It is the treatment given by our God. But I am not the equal of a priest." She replaced the cloth on Naabak's forehead. Heat clung to the linen. Even the water was warm. And dirty.

"You know more than all of us," Gil said in a half-conscious moan.

Naabak gazed at her. She tried to give him a reassuring smile, but it was devoured by threats of death.

"Seek the God of Moses. The hour is late and Hadad has not answered your prayers." She shooed a fly from Naabak's eye.

"If Hadad wills—"

She fisted the bed sheet. "Call out to my God."

"He is not mine." Naabak turned his face from her. A pool of rose-colored sweat wetted the cloth underneath his head.

And look what your god has done. Nothing. Her pulse drummed down to her fingertips. "What if another god triumphs over Hadad? You have fought many battles and won. What if there was a god with your prowess? One who is mightier than all the others?"

"Your God," Naabak gurgled.

"Yes." Her voice rang out with a righteous fervor. She dipped a sponge in the insect-infested water. "Come with me to Mahanaim. To see the prophet. To seek a new life." She wiped a drip trickling down his swollen cheek. "Win this last battle."

His eyes closed. "It is too late, Israel."

"Then it is too late for me." She wrung out the cloth not caring if leprosy overtook her pores. Without Naabak she would not live long. Without Gil, she would not care to live.

15

A moan rumbled from Gil's lips as she tied a bandage around his arm.

"You have treated that wound." Gil tried to stretch out his body. He looked as agile as her elderly aunt.

"I have nothing to clean it with, but this will slow the bleeding. If the skin is pulled together, it may not scar."

"What is one more mark?" He flinched at her touch.

"I should warn you. My father would pronounce me unclean. I have touched Naabak's rags."

Gil's grunt became a snorted laugh. "Heathens have handled me all day. I lived in their filth. *Adonai* will have to overlook our transgressions. Do not stop. I was dreaming of your touch. Now I wake to find my dream has come true."

A wave of desire filled her belly. "You should not speak of such things. We are not alone."

"I will shout it in the fields. Without hindrance." His voice grew louder. "I have found a wife." His breath warmed her nose. "I can give you more children than that old priest."

If she could have voiced a reply without feeling wanton, she would have encouraged his passion. She wanted to fall asleep on him and feel his strength, his warmth. But they were in captivity, awaiting Konath's wrath.

"It would be a blessing to give you a child and to watch your mother hold your babe." She curled into his chest, careful not to press into his bruises. "Though I doubt I will even bear one child. I will perish here in Aram." She glanced at the jagged rock cave. "This is our last resting place."

"My mother has her husband's sons to fill her lap." The weight of his chin pressed against her head covering. "I care only to fill your lap, and I shall make it so."

The desire in his words delighted her. Oh, if she could only have his strength and vision.

She looked into Gil's battered face. "You are your mother's flesh and blood. A son she is proud to call her own. She told me you were a good man. You would help me in my time of need. I have seen that goodness tenfold."

Gil's head rocked side to side against his stone backrest. "Do not tell anyone here. I have worked hard at my troublesome reputation." His voice held a subdued tease.

She snuggled against his bandaged arm. Only a little scarlet stained the wrap. That was good. The sweet fellowship of being with Gil weighed on her eyelids. A brief nap would cause no harm.

After what seemed like an hour of restful sleep, Hannah woke to threats traveling down the corridor. She knew that agitated, know-it-all, Moabite voice.

Mereb appeared in the doorway. He slapped at the hesitant servants, urging them forward into the room with their large jars of water. A slave held a tray at arm's length like the bronze was already diseased. Mereb pushed the slaves forward, barking directions from a cautious distance. It seemed Reumah had honored her requests for clothing and aloes.

Naabak did not acknowledge the visitors. He stared at the ceiling as if bewitched by the stone.

Gil's head balanced on his bent knees. He was either unconcerned with Mereb's interruption or in a deep sleep. She rose and directed the slaves where to place the supplies. Had Reumah come to her senses? Was she willing to save her husband and her position?

"Provisions from the house." Mereb opened his arms as though he were welcoming her to a banquet.

"Do not expect gratitude from me. You are a wicked man who betrays women." She clenched her teeth to keep from spewing more mockery.

Mereb stood his dirt. "I bring you food, water, and clothing, and this is how you greet me? With hatred?"

"Is it time to throw me into another pit?" The memory of lust-fueled hands assaulting her was like a serpent crawling over her skin.

Mereb crossed his arms against the sheen of his damask sash. "Did you not seek him?" He pointed a finger at Gil. "If he is your husband, it is I who should be angry. Your soiled virginity would have been learned by the advisor's loins."

Her heart hammered against her chest. She restrained her rage, not wanting to wake Naabak with her wailing. She had not lied to Mereb initially, and she would not undo the lie that had saved Gil's life. Another fist in Mereb's nose would be righteous revenge. "What allegiance do I owe to you? Have you not sent me into danger at the house, at the temple, and in this mountain?"

"Hah." Mereb's head rocked backward. "Did I not send Reumah to find you?" His voice lowered. "If you had not insisted on saving your man, you would be asleep on your mat."

"Only after a beating for refusing to unite with a pagan priest." Voicing the events made her feel even more corrupted. "You forced me forward."

Gil flinched at her confession. He began to rise.

Mereb started and turned to leave. "Wash your filth. Our mistress will return in the morning. She is expecting a miracle from your herbs. And from you."

"My wife." Naabak rolled onto his side. "Does she desire my healing?"

"We all do." Hannah gave Gil a raised-eyebrow look that insisted he stay silent.

"This had better not be a trick," Mereb uttered under his breath.

"These remedies come from God's law." She fisted her hands. "I assure you it is not a game."

Turning from Mereb, she rushed to attend to Naabak's sores. She poured fresh water in a basin and scrubbed all the way from her fingers to her elbows. How she wished she could submerge her whole body and be ceremonially clean. But bathing before she handled Naabak's flesh was useless and a waste of their precious water.

Tearing the hyssop leaves into pieces, she swirled them in a jar.

"Do you not fear illness?" Naabak asked, his eyes intent on her preparations.

"I am confident the hyssop that cures your infection will protect my skin as well." Bending over the bed, she loosened his burlap-colored bandages. *Oh, to have a fire to burn these in.*

Naabak shuddered as his flesh clung to the cloth.

"The sap from the leaves should soothe your

skin," she added to calm his apprehension.

"You put too much faith in this ritual." Tremors shook the commander's body as if her hands were spiked blades.

She placed a wetted cloth on his stubbed feet. "The faith I have is in my God and His Law. But you must rest your mouth. When I am done tending you, our meal shall be cool enough to eat." For a moment, she envisioned herself back in Jerusalem, serving her father and mother. Her days away from home seemed like years. Would her family still accept her after all the strife she had caused?

"It is stew." Gil held the pot's lid in his hand. "The meat is pork."

Her stomach argued for its portion. "Are you certain?"

Gil breathed in deep. "Yes. With *nana*. Mint." He held out two bowls. "I will take out our portions before you dip the commander's bread. It may do little good, but his open flesh will make the meal unclean."

A grunt of humor came from Naabak's throat.

"But the meat is forbidden. The pig does not chew its cud. We cannot eat of it." Warmth flushed her face.

She rinsed her hands and broke off a piece of bread for herself. Wrapping it in clean linen, she placed it in her lap.

"You must eat," Gil warned.

"Bread is enough." Her stomach gurgled painfully as the stew broth seeped into the bread she fed to Naabak. She would not defile herself by consuming an animal God had forbidden His people to eat.

"Bread alone will be like chewing papyrus." Gil gave her a knowing glance.

"If it pokes my mouth like your mutton, all is

well."

"Have some," Naabak said. "It is good." His tongue moistened what was left of his lips.

Her shoulders slumped, submerging Naabak's bread deeper into the stew. Should she turn from the laws of God for a savory stew? Had she not incurred judgment already? The list of her sins weighed on her conscience. In one day, she had entered the temple of a foreign god, kissed a man's lips in lust—a man who was not her husband—lied about her relationship with Gil, burned with anger, touched a pagan's open wounds, and even now, her fingers wetted in the juices of a filthy animal. Why would the prophet hear her plea on behalf of Naabak? He wouldn't hear her plea on behalf of herself.

"Daughter of Zebula, do you not have any thoughts for me?" Gil eased down beside her. One would not know his bowl had ever held pork. He reached across and tore off the heel of bread. "I washed," he said, indicating the tall jars. "My hands are clean." The brush of his confession was upon her ear. "Do not judge me harshly for my body is weak."

Gil retreated to the far corner. His absence left her skin chilled.

Her chest tightened as if the bread had caught in her windpipe. She pressed Naabak's palms against a wine goblet and helped him drink with as much dignity as a decaying man could possess. She stacked the dishes by the water jars. A small cedar-carved idol rested near the base. It was Hadad. Was this one of Mereb's schemes? She had asked for cedar, not a graven image. She flung the flaming-eyed false god into the hallway. "It is unclean."

As her voice rang in her ears, she remembered the

crowd in Jerusalem proclaiming her defilement. If they only knew how far she had fallen.

The guard glared in her direction.

"Strips or blocks of cedar are best. An idol is of no use to me. Or your commander." She nodded reverently at the soldier.

After Naabak drained his goblet, she knelt in front of Gil.

Tears flooded her eyes. "Never will I judge you. When you left Jerusalem with me, I did not mean for you to be afflicted. Struck by the enemy. I am responsible for your wounds and your hunger. And if the prophet does not heal Naabak, or if God takes his life in the desert..." Her vowels broke like shattered pottery. "Will your death not be because of me?"

"Hannah." He spoke her name in a melody that washed over her soul. "You could not have kept me from this venture." He stroked her arms. "You did not hide in my bedroom by accident. On that day, the providence of God brought you into my life. He brought you to me. You, a girl in need of mercy and healing. How could I sit and do nothing?" His caress rose to her cheek. "I do not regret it."

A thin creek of tears streamed down her face. She brushed them aside in awe of this man. Gil did not care about his surroundings, her curse, not even death.

Lifting his hand from her face, she kissed his scarred palm and cradled it like it was a most treasured possession. "It was not wholly your bedroom," she said, carefully poking his chest. "And it is my duty as the daughter of a priest to uphold our laws. My father and brother make atonement for our people."

"We have no tabernacle here to make atonement."

Gil grabbed her hands. "I promise. We will atone when we return to Jerusalem."

"If we return," she said.

"Where is your faith? Our return to Jerusalem will be met with the harp and lyre and singing." He drew closer. "We will bring gold and silver from Aram."

"Now you jest." She pulled away.

"Do I, Commander?"

Gil and Naabak assessed each other as soldiers meeting on the battlefield.

"If our God were to heal you, are we not free from your bondage? Free to go back to our city? Our families?"

Naabak adjusted his legs in the bed. "If," he stressed with a huffing sound, "I am restored, you may return to your city."

"And we would have coin for our return?" Gil's cadence quickened as if he were closing a deal in trade.

Hannah shivered at Gil's boldness.

"Enough." Naabak batted a sponge from the bed.

She retrieved the sponge, wetted it, and replaced it on Naabak's forehead. Fever still plagued him. Was his promise a delusion?

Gil struggled to his feet. "Come and wash." He held out his hand. "Cleanse yourself and you will be settled."

Her gaze darted to Gil, to Naabak, and then to the door.

"I cannot wash in the flesh, naked to men's eyes." The guard in the threshold looked in her direction.

Gil unfurled a clean sheet. His arms stayed shoulder height. He stood with his back to Naabak and the guard. "The weave is tight. I will not see you."

"Are you able to hold the cloth without pain? I do

not want it falling when I am bare. Or you to bleed."
Her heart raced as she thought of removing her dress
with men just a few feet away.

"Trust your husband." The tease in his voice
tugged at her mouth. "I will not let strangers gaze
upon the nakedness that is meant for me."

She strolled to the nearest jar. One step. Two steps.
Three steps. Gil followed.

Did she have the boldness to strip off her clothes?
She had requested the water from Reumah. Enough
was brought for both drinking and purification. In
order to be right with Hebrew law, she would have to
bathe.

Gil raised the linen. He looked amused at her
predicament. "They can only gaze upon your feet."

"You use too many words," Naabak said with
groggy agitation.

Slipping out of the once-fine tunic Reumah had
provided to entice the pagan priest, Hannah washed
off the day's defilement, sweat, mud, and blood. She
dipped her hair in the water and wrung it out, letting a
few drops drain down her back.

*Oh, Adonai, may Reumah come to this cave in the
morning. Revive her husband this night.*

The bed sheet quaked near the top where Gil had
hold. She remembered his wounded arm.

"I am hurrying." Slipping into her new tunic was
like a bath in oil of myrrh. She ran her hand over the
cloth and admired the flow of the skirt.

"My turn." Gil dropped the sheet.

"How did you know I was ready?" Her eyes
questioned him.

"The lamp creates an outline. You will see the
shadows when it is your turn." He handed her the bed

sheet.

What would she see? More importantly, what had he seen?

The sheet dampened where she held it.

"I am smaller than you. I should turn around?"

Gil steadied himself on the lip of the tall vessel. "Hold it in front of your face. My scars need not be on display. Again." The displeasure of the pit could be heard in his voice.

She pulled the cloth taut in front of her eyes and shut her eyelids tight, concentrating on the darkness.

Minutes passed. Her arms burned from their sculpted pose. Her thumb cramped. She wiggled her fingers.

The sheet dipped.

Her eyes flew open.

She saw.

She righted the sheet.

"I felt a draft," Gil said, amused.

No answer came. No way would she confess to seeing his backside. His very clean, muscular backside.

If she and Gil ever got out of this mountain and made it to Mahanaim, not only would she have to convince the prophet to heal an enemy army commander, she would have to confess to a lengthy list of transgressions.

But, she thought, with a lick of her lips, what was one more transgression? After all, she had proclaimed to men in authority that Gil was her husband. She had to make the lie seem truthful. She had to act as if gazing upon him was commonplace.

So, quickly and quietly, she sneaked another peek.

Gil's head whipped around. His eyebrows shot upward. She hid her face in the sheet and tried to block out   his   amused   chuckle.

16

Hours later, Gil still wore the grin of a lone child rewarded with a cup of sweet milk. Hannah had been tending Naabak's fever. His forehead was warm now. Not scalding.

"How is he?" Reumah crossed the threshold, but hesitated to approach the bed.

Hannah scrambled to her feet. She looked to the hall for Konath. No surge of anger rallied her body. She was too tired to hate this early in the morning.

"You're alone?" The words came forth before she could temper their insinuation.

"Mereb is at the house." Reumah sounded surprised. "My servants and I have offered prayers for my husband. I have come for Naabak's ring. To send for letters from the King of Aram. Do we not need royal decree to cross into your holy land?" Reumah jutted her chin in queenly fashion. Wetness glistened on her cheeks. She stepped cautiously toward her husband. Her gown swept the floor. She was draped and jeweled like the perfect temptress. "Surely the king owes us one last favor."

Naabak clutched at a pouch hanging from his neck. If he had been whole, it would have been ripped from his chest for all his eagerness.

Hannah dropped to her knees and untied the leather-stringed knot for her master. Her fingers trembled. Her whole body shivered, overcome with delight at the possibility of returning to her homeland. Did Naabak finally believe her? Believe the prophet in Israel could heal his disease? *As well as mine.*

"Susa is loyal." Naabak rasped. "Send him with my ring and authority to Damascus."

Not Konath?

Loosening the drawstring, she let the gold signet ring fall onto a clean bandage. The cloth hung like a sling from her fingers. She offered the gold band, a sign of her last hope, to Reumah. Reumah clutched it to her breast. Perhaps, the ring was her last hope, too.

~*~

Two days passed. Hannah uncovered Naabak's sores. Fewer gnats came. Fewer appendages reddened. Supporting her master's neck, she forced him to drink clean water.

Gil paced like a corralled lion. The small room couldn't compare to vast open fields or winding city alleys.

She prayed for freedom at the designated hours for temple prayer. At times, her strength faltered. She feared being lost to her family and Gil. Gil joined her on bended knee, in the morning, in the afternoon, and in the dark of night.

Letters finally came for passage across the border into Israel. God had answered her request. Her petition had not failed. At least not this time.

After two days, she emerged from the shadows of the mountain. Breaths of wind-swept air emboldened her spirit. Her head covering shielded her eyes from the blaze of the unspent sun. She walked through the arena. Tears wetted her cheeks, but not from sorrow. In a day's time, she and Gil would set foot in Israel, in the Promised Land.

She would make good on her word to Naabak to seek the prophet and witness a miracle. First, the healing of Naabak. Then, a healing for herself. Naabak had saved her life not once, but twice. She was indebted to her master for sparing Gil's life, too.

Gil, Benjamin, and two pit dwellers carried Naabak from his stone prison. Each gripped a corner of a mat and shuffled toward a bed, set high on a wheeled cart with cloth walls and a cloth ceiling. Soldiers parted as the withered commander neared.

"How many more days must I suffer this humiliation?" Naabak asked as Gil and Benjamin lifted him onto the sheets.

She beheld his bandaged face. "These two days have made you stronger for the journey. Your flesh is not scarlet. And these walls"—she tugged on the linen—"Will keep the dirt and maggots at bay."

"What good is a man who cannot hold a cup or produce an heir?" Naabak said.

Gil bent at the waist. "If he commands advancing armies, it is a blessing."

Naabak huffed. His wounds and his imprisonment had drained his strength, but not his allegiance.

"Does your mouth ever stay shut, Hebrew?" Naabak used his elbows to rise up in the bed.

"It will be over soon enough." She rolled up the soiled mat.

"You do not comfort me, Israel, unless you refer to your prophet's power." Naabak shot her an accusatory stare.

"I do," she added quickly.

"As do I," Reumah said. She sat in a similarly extravagant cart with grand wheels and whitewashed emblems. Her silk gown and veils, the color of powdered malachite, billowed in the hint of a breeze. Her traveling throne bathed in the shade of the lone fig tree growing a few feet from the idol-embedded archway. Mereb secured supplies in the back of her wagon.

Hannah waved at Reumah and Mereb. A satisfied smile graced her lips. Mereb's extra chores were fitting for his betrayals.

Konath emerged from behind a formation of foot soldiers.

"Throw the slaves back in the pit."

Panic jarred her heart like a dice roll. "Not all? Not my husband? I need him to find the city."

Gil clung to Naabak's cart. He searched for a path of escape. Every alley led to a soldier of Aram or a manned chariot.

Konath unsheathed his sword. He let the sun glimmer off his blade.

"We already know our way across the border. You dogs will die before your first leprous sore."

"Your men speak Aramaic not Hebrew." Her words were meant for Konath, but she looked directly into Naabak's crusted eyes. She gripped Gil's arm to keep her knees steady.

"You speak Hebrew." Konath rotated the tip of his weapon closer to Gil's chest.

"But no foreign dialects. The men of Manasseh have Egyptian blood." Sweat pooled above her lip. "Will they listen to a woman who babbles?" She would not cast off Gil and sentence him to a slow slaughter.

"We will need the other Hebrew guest as well."

Gil spoke as if Konath had agreed to his company. "He is from the tribe of Manasseh."

Did Gil know no fear? She was trying to save his life and now he added another demand? She looked at the indentations surrounding Benjamin's ribs. The scabs on his face. He had fought bravely in the pit to halt her undoing. Her conscience would not leave him to ruin.

"Who is this tribe that I should be concerned with them?" Konath's voice shook with anger.

Gil stepped forward. "A great commander plans victory not defeat." His insult rang out over the troops.

Konath lunged at Gil and backhanded his face. Blood seeped from Gil's lip.

Veins ridged Gil's taut muscles.

"He speaks the truth." She spoke boldly like a judge. "The city of Mahanaim is a holy city. The land belongs to the tribe of Levi, but the hills are patrolled by the tribe of Manasseh. They mix Egyptian vowels with their Hebrew." She turned to Naabak. "Master, they are sharp-witted fighters."

"Bind her husband's hands." Naabak spoke with authority and loud enough for his officers to hear. "He will not abandon his wife. If there is truth in what they say, he will be useful. Bring the other and secure a place for them in the front lines for all of Manasseh to see."

"Lord, what does a girl know of such things?" Konath lowered his voice, but he did not step closer to his commander. His cadence was as smooth as eastern silks. "This Jew seeks for us to taunt Israel. Will not war follow?"

She leaned over the planked side of Naabak's bed and touched his arm. "Master, I am no soldier. I seek only peace and healing. May no blood be upon my hands, nor yours."

Naabak glanced at Konath and then turned his attention to Hannah. She did not look away from his deformity, but searched his gaze for the man he once was.

"Bring the rope." Naabak sputtered and coughed from the force of his demand.

"Heed your commander's orders," Konath shouted to two foot soldiers. He turned and assessed her form, slowly, seductively. She shivered as if she had jumped into the River Jordan.

"You play pious well. But you will not win." His mumbled words reached her ears alone.

Konath strode toward the line of chariots and assumed command. Maybe he thought by the end of this trip, he would be in charge of Aram's forces.

A soldier knotted a rope around Gil's wrists. Hannah's bones hollowed as if the marrow had drained to her feet. Gil was no common thief. He was an honest man captured in an illegal raid. But if this humiliation would spare his life, she would bind him herself.

Gil winced at the final cinch.

When the soldier stepped away to bind Benjamin's fists, she secured a covering on Gil's head with a strip of linen. "This will keep the sweat from your eyes and the sun from your skin. May our people recognize you as one of their own." She brushed the side of his face and thumbed the blood from his mouth. Touching him gave her soul flight.

Gil let the weight of his jaw rest in her hand. "You will be safe in the center of the caravan," he whispered. "If our brothers, the men of Manasseh come, you must hide. Call out to our people to protect you. Let them know you are a Hebrew captured by the enemy."

"And what of you at the front by Konath's side?" Her throat tightened as though tied with twine.

"My soul will be at peace knowing you are safe on our land." Gil straightened.

She took his hands and stroked his wrists, massaging the skin under the scratchy ropes. "You cannot leave me. Not even in death. If you do—" Her voice squeaked as her lungs constricted. "I will not find rest." *And I will not find another.* She glanced at Naabak's decaying body. "But do not think ill of me if I do not slip away when the soldiers of Manasseh come to meet us. I owe a debt to Naabak. If the prophet is near, I will beseech him to heal the commander."

"Is it an oath that binds you?" Gil's stance went rigid.

"I will not break the laws of a vow, and I have vowed that the prophet can heal him. He travels at my urging. How can I watch him be slaughtered? Would I not be responsible for taking a life?"

"What binds you to me? Who am I that my death should have concerned you for more than a sunrise? I am the offspring of a man that defiled an innocent woman in the gleaning fields." He spoke as if he believed that lie.

Her bones trembled. "I will not listen to such slander. There is good blood in you. You escorted me out of Jerusalem and through the wilderness at great risk to your name."

"Another man would have done the same."

She shook her head. "No." Her throat grew reed thin as tears welled in her eyes. Choking out her truth, she said, "You did not turn me out onto the street when you found me in your dwelling place. You shared your food and you stood up to my brother as if I was worth your trouble, worth something. No one has ever done that for me save my father and mother. I will not lose you, Gilead." She looked into the depths of his brown eyes. "My husband." Her heartfelt declaration hung in the air. "You have the boldness of seven kings."

Gil shuffled forward and tipped her chin with his finger. He seemed taller, broader. "You give me the confidence of ten kings. And if you will not run, then stay close to Naabak's shield and the letters from the palace. Pray whatever prayers your father recites in the temple. For the men of Manasseh will come out to meet the armies of Aram."

The caress of his finger filled her with a fleeting hope. She and Gil may have been God's people, chosen and set apart, but this day they were aligned with an enemy of Israel.

A soldier jerked on Gil's tunic. He pulled Gil from her grasp and pushed him toward the front of the caravan.

Benjamin mouthed, "*Shalom.*"

She sank to her knees and prayed.

Hear, O Israel: The Lord is our God, the Lord alone.

When she looked up, Gil had vanished amidst the fighting men of Aram.

Hear, O Israel: The Lord is our God...and you Lord have cursed me. If you hear my petitions, heed this request.

Restore Naabak. But I beg you to rescue my Gil.

17

Hannah threw Naabak's uneaten lamb into the fire. Cinders sparked then blackened the meat to ash. The constant tromp of hooves, wheels, and footfalls had ceased, and only the occasional cadence of orders rang into the night. Darkness hid the sculpted cliffs that marked the entrance to her homeland.

The longing in her heart remained. Longing for Gil. Longing for her family and for her city. Why had God allowed her capture? Wasn't she seeking the mouthpiece of God in the land of the Levites?

"I have been faithful all my life," she muttered to a winking star. "Do not abandon me when I have come so far in search of your prophet."

The crush of pebbles startled her.

"I knew you to be mad. Shrewd, but mad." Konath knelt by the fire and glanced toward Naabak's cart. "And what of our commander?"

"He lives." She drew back from the heat of the flames. And from him. One swift move and he could drag her into the darkness.

"Pity. Death would spare us a battle."

His laugh rippled along her skin snake-charming the hairs on her neck and arms.

"You have breached this border before." She switched the subject from death. "Did you not leave any plunder?"

"There will be spoils." The sweep of his gaze toward Reumah's bedchamber caused Hannah's throat to gag. "And sport. Your husband may be able to fight one or two of my men, but a dozen? His flesh will feed the vultures from here to Damascus."

Spit pooled in her mouth. The desire to slap his face wooed her. She swallowed the temptation. "You are wicked. Do you not fear God? The men of Manasseh?"

"Who is the wicked one? You tease me and run for refuge. Interrupt my pleasures. Snatch sport from my arena. Plot schemes with my commander." He stalked around her like a hunter until his breath bathed her face. "Soon, I will answer to the King of Aram. No one else. Not your false god."

"That is blasphemy." She ducked from the cage of his body, nearer to Reumah's cart.

He blocked her path.

"I have been in wait for this command for too long. I am as great as Naabak. Have I not risen to fame in his absence? He is diseased. He must let go of his life."

"You boast while Naabak suffers? What a vile man." She spit forth the truth.

Konath chuckled. He beat his chest, reveling in the decay of his commander.

"I fear Reumah will not be enough for me when I am second to the King. I will be in need of concubines."

She dodged the stroke of his fat fingers. "I may be contagious."

He held his ground. "You look healthy."

"I would die first."

"How about you die after?" Konath's seductive

smirk was a millstone in her belly.

Doubling back, she ran to the safety of Naabak's infirmary. Sitting cross-legged in the corner of his bed frame, she gripped the planked oak. She scraped the wood grain with her thumbnail, willing her heart not to burst forth through her ribs. Naabak's cart was her anchor in Konath's savage storm.

Aramean phrases filtered from Reumah's cart chamber. Hannah recognized Konath's hiss. She recognized Reumah's silky excuses. Hannah did not understand all the foreign bickering or the guttural threats. She did understand Reumah's final word to Konath. "No."

Hannah had not realized she had fallen asleep until the *ah-wooh* summons of a ram's horn jolted her awake.

Naabak struggled to right himself. A cloth fell from his forehead.

Horse hooves drummed the ground, clopping closer.

"Commander," a man shouted.

Hannah whipped open the drape. Her eyes flickered from dawn's light and a newly disturbed cloud of dirt.

"Men are waiting in the valley. Archers lurk in the cliffs," the soldier's alert rushed from his mouth.

"Strength?" Naabak asked.

"One hundred men on the ground."

"Weapons?" Naabak rocked forward. No fear or surprise agitated his voice.

"Swords. Spears. Bows. Arrows. Shields." The soldier's gaze did not move from Naabak as the weapons were recited.

"Do they have horses? Chariots?"

The soldier shook his head. "None to speak of. The leader and a few men have mounts."

"Do they fear us?" Naabak tented the sheet with his knees. It appeared he contemplated leaving the cart.

The soldier did not shrink away from Naabak's deformities. "Some. Most seem confident. The Hebrew slave has called out across the lines."

"Your men have come to greet us." Naabak set his gaze on Hannah's face.

She squelched the pride billowing in her chest. "You doubted their steadfastness. They will die protecting the land God gave them. Gave us." Her people were not any different than the Arameans. But the men of Aram not only protected their borders, they raided to expand them.

"We seek your prophet, not bloodshed. They will respect the King's letters?" There was a hint of question in Naabak's statement.

She leaned closer to Naabak, her pride bursting forth. "My people are just."

A choked dismissal came from the soldier.

She threw a wad of bandages his direction.

He ducked and stepped backward. His shadow grew smaller on the cloth wall.

"You must go to the front, Israel." Naabak turned to the soldier. "And not due to her aim." She thought she saw Naabak's mouth quiver. "Her husband will speak to the enemy for us. He will not jeopardize her life. The cost is too high if he betrays us."

Would Naabak's confidence in Gil be so steadfast if he knew she and Gil were not married? Gil was a fighting man of Judah, a Hebrew before all else.

She wetted a cloth and placed it in Naabak's palm.

"For when I am gone."

After mounting the soldier's spirited mare, she righted her head covering. The men and priests of Mahanaim did not need to know she was cursed. The Damascus holy pattern on her tunic would be offensive enough.

She assessed Naabak's army. Rows of sword-ready men stood by chariots. All looked ready to devour the enemy. How had it come to this? She wanted to be right with God, not start a war. Her father had been diligent in his petitions for healing, but the prophet had turned her away. Turned his back on the line of Zebula. What would her life be like this day if the man of God had healed her curses? Would she have crossed paths with Gil? And if not, could she have found happiness with another? Gil consumed her thoughts, her feelings, her being. She did not want to dwell on a life without him.

Konath sat perched on a stallion. His front line spanned the width of the valley. He was flanked by two men. Susa, the soldier Naabak had sent to Damascus, accompanied Konath on his right side. The tormentor from the arena rode on Konath's left side. She searched for Gil. Her heart sped. Where was he? She dismounted and weaved her way to Konath.

The leader of Manasseh's forces trotted his horse forward.

A reverent silence descended on the valley as if life or death would be declared in the words that followed.

"What scheme of Aram brings you across our border?" the warrior shouted. He edged his horse under a battered acacia tree for cover. "Does not enough of our blood drip from your swords?"

Konath consulted his armor bearer.

Gil and Benjamin were led out from the ranks.

Relief flooded her limbs. They were alive and had not been cast off.

Gil and Benjamin wore embroidered tunics, bold in color with bronze rivets in their belts. How crafty of Konath to hide the stripes on their chests. They were no longer tied like sheep at shearing time.

Gil strolled into the expanse separating the two armies. Benjamin followed, along with a guard.

Gil raised his hands as if he planned to embrace all of Manasseh's men. "Aram seeks the prophet of Israel," he shouted. "Shall we deny them the wisdom of *Adonai*?"

Her brow furrowed. She knew most of Gil's Hebrew but stumbled over a few words.

"Look." Gil urged Benjamin forward, closer to the ranks of his kin. "They have brought you one of your own. He is free to return to his people."

The soldier on Konath's left balked at Gil's offering.

The leader of Manasseh raised his sword. Gilded silver shone in the sunlight, but the weapon was not as fine as the blades of Aram. Yet, it would slay a man in earnest.

"What do pagans know of our God? What is He to them? You are spies. Your King sets a trap for the innocent." The leader of Manasseh kicked his horse and pulled hard on the reins. The Chestnut reared up as its rider slashed at the air with his sword. "Turn back. You are not welcome in this valley or beyond."

"If they want a fight," Konath said to the men at his sides, "we will rout them."

"No." She would not have innocent blood on her hands.

Konath turned. His eyes bulged like a beast ready to devour. "Tie her—"

She ran, swift of foot, into the deserted space.

Gil yelled. She did not heed him. Rocks numbed her toes. She sought the leader of Manasseh. No one else.

The wind threatened to rip off her head covering and humiliate her. She held the muslin tight. Her breath burned her throat. If an arrow felled her, she would die trying to save innocent lives. Gil's life. Benjamin's life.

She slowed her sprint as she neared the acacia tree. The leader did not leave his shade. Dropping to the ground, she bowed low. Crushed rock pained her knees. Warm soil flushed her forehead.

"If you are angry, then the fault lies with me. I, Hannah *bat* Zebula have sung praises of the Creator to our pagan neighbors. Am I wrong? Does our God not send the rain on Aram as well as Israel? If blood is shed this day, it will be on the hands of Manasseh and Levi. For I have drawn Aram here to the city of the Levites for an audience with the prophet."

The leader moved into the light. "How is this?"

Hannah shielded her eyes from the sun's glare. The leader's cocked head and unyielding stare beseeched her to finish.

She stayed low. "My master is in need of healing. As am I. The house of Zebula knows the prophet by name. My father and brother have spoken with the Anointed One face to face. Another meeting with him is all I ask."

The Chestnut's head bobbed. Hooves retreated from her body, taking a sliver of shade with them.

"Why should the need of Aram concern me?"

In truth, it shouldn't. She owed a debt to Naabak, not to this man. Oh, to have some of Gil's outspokenness now.

"Vengeance." She spit the word from her mouth like a pit. "If you crush the King's men, will he not send more? Will the Ammonites not side with Aram and flood our land? You will give them reason to hate us more than they already do."

He assessed his army. "How do I know you speak the truth and are not the King's concubine?"

Her gut hollowed. The thrumming in her ears mimicked the march of troops.

"Shall I recite the *Shema*? The Commandments? The Levitical Law?" Her voice trembled. How dare he accuse her of being a heathen! "Name whatever tradition you want spoken. I am a chief priest's daughter and have remained true to my people."

She rose to her feet and fisted her hands on her hips.

He gazed upon her. And Gil. And Benjamin.

Had he understood her rant? What else could she say? *Think.*

A surge of hope flooded her body. "I know the prophet's name."

The leader grinned as if he thought her a fool. "He is known over all of Israel and Judah."

"But I can write his name." Hannah ran to the tree and snapped off a spindly branch. Standing with her back to the leader, she drew the letters that named the prophet, tracing over the wobble of her first mark.

Right to left.

Perfect Hebrew.

The Hebrew her father had written the day of her humiliation.

She turned and sought the leader's affirmation. He studied her face. Her eyes burned and watered, but she would not close them. He finally nodded.

"Sweep it away and release our brother from captivity."

As she erased the etching, she asked, "You will let us pass into Mahanaim?"

"Mahanaim is of no use to you."

"I do not understand." She wet her cracked lips with a dry tongue. Was her translation in error? "We need to see the prophet."

He glanced into the clouds above the cliffs. "The prophet is not in the city. He has gone up the mountain to speak with God."

She looked up at the deep, sloping crags. Trails cut into those cliffs would be narrow and strewn with rocks. The acacia branch fell from her fingertips. Naabak would have to be carried up that mountain, to the prophet, before he died. Wiping the dust from her hands, she turned toward Aram's forces. At least this time she traveled outside the mountain.

18

Hannah walked in the shade of the Chestnut alongside the leader of the tribe of Manasseh, Makir *ben* Gamaliel. If only he could have ridden in front of her as a shield from the penetrating stares of Konath's soldiers. Judgment crossed their helmet-fortified faces. Judgment as from the crowd in Jerusalem. Unclean? Cursed? Traitor? Spy? Her skin burned hot and tingled like the time she grasped a fork from the fire.

Makir reined in his mount a maneuverable distance from Konath.

"The one you seek has gone up the mountain to talk with God." Makir spoke forthright. "It is commonplace with one such as him."

Konath cackled like a wild dog calling its pack. His men assessed his reaction. So did she. No one smirked. She flexed her fingers behind her back and remained stalwart. Facing Konath was easier with the army of Israel at her side.

"It is a trick," Konath roared. "A trick to separate me from my men and murder me on the rock."

"It is easier to rout you here," Gil said from his position next to Benjamin. "And spill more of Aram's blood."

Konath's armor grew more intimidating with the swell of his chest. He stepped closer to Gil.

"Lord Konath," she interrupted. She shuddered at

the address, but sparing Gil another attack was foremost in her thoughts. Her hope had been dwindling like a beggar's candle. "It seems the prophet left yesterday at first light. The time of his return is uncertain."

Makir nodded an affirmation to her testimony.

She rolled her shoulders back and let the fancy-patterned linen give her the illusion of height. "I am not afraid to take my master up the mountain. Your King wished as much."

Konath's stallion bucked its head at its tightening reins. "Our master has no hands or feet. Will you drag him in the dust?"

"You would allow death because your commander is late?" Makir questioned. "Let him decide if our God is the Most High God. Will the journey not determine his fate?"

And mine? With the look Konath gave her, she shuddered to think of her end if Naabak perished.

Gil stepped forward. "I will carry him. I am not afraid of illness or ambush."

Makir nodded favorably to Gil. "The path is wide enough for a small ass."

"We have one of those." Gil rested his hand on Mereb's shoulder and exchanged a brotherly wink with Benjamin.

Hannah stifled any hint of a smile, any twitch. Too much was at stake to provoke Konath.

"And if we set up camp," Konath said, no folly in his tone, "will my men suffer death by your arrows?"

"Not before your chariots slay some of my men." Makir edged his mount forward. "Stay and we will swear a truce. May this valley not be defiled by bloodshed."

Oh Lord, do not add the slaughter of men to my list of transgressions.

Reumah strolled forward. Her bright veils and jewels budded with life. She was a lily in a field of sweat-stained leather and dented armor. She bent a knee and displayed a bob of respect. "My husband and all of Aram will be in your debt."

"It is the mountain to which you will owe a debt," Makir said. He ignored Konath's stalwart stance. His attention stayed on Reumah.

"I skirted the catacombs of Helbon as a child. This mountain is a foothold to me." Reumah lifted her arm toward the cliffs. Bracelets clinked and molded into a mass of gold.

Hannah joined Reumah and dipped her head in a show of respect. "Will you bestow a guide?" Hannah asked Makir. The sooner they got on their way, the better.

"Gather your party and I will lead you to the base of the mountain." Makir motioned for Benjamin to join him.

Reumah did not waiver.

Konath did not object.

"There is one path and one path alone. Do not veer to the left or to the right," Makir said.

Benjamin practically leapt onto Makir's horse. "Your wife is a brave woman, Gilead. You must receive me if I venture south."

If Benjamin only knew how her bones quaked. "I will wash your feet in the City of David," she said in earnest. If she and Gil made it down the mountain alive.

Hannah hurried to check on Naabak and prepare for the trip. As she neared Naabak's cart, Mereb stepped from behind the cloth wall.

"It is your fault our mistress desires to climb the mountain," Mereb said. "You have filled her head with Hebrew mysticism."

"What do you know of my heritage? I could curse you in Hebrew and you would be none the wiser." She pushed the Moabite away and walked on, making a list in her head of bandages and hyssop leaves. Not that her herbs would make Naabak new, only God could restore Naabak's body. The dancing boy in Jerusalem was proof of God's healing power. But following the Levitical laws for clean skin couldn't hurt her master's chances.

"Do not fool with me." Mereb's words were a wind at her back. "Trouble came to this household with your arrival."

She whipped around. "I did not wish to come to Aram and remain in captivity. Your lies have kindled Konath's hatred."

"And your lies have brought false hope and travel to the land of the enemy." Mereb kicked at the hard ground.

"Who is the enemy?" Gil came up beside Mereb. Susa, the guard who had retrieved the letters from the King of Aram, trailed behind him. "Are we not accompanying the King's commander?"

"A strong back is all I need from you," Mereb said, his gaze barely skimming Gil's face.

"If you're the other back, then I truly am the one in need." Gil's laughter caused the guard to crack a smile. How could Gil chide after all the beatings he had endured?

"I have my mistress to attend to." Mereb shrugged off Gil's goading.

Reumah opened the linen drape around her bed. "Swaddle another. This trip is nothing to me. It is a one way stroll. My husband can attend to me on the way down."

Mereb bent low at Reumah's voice. Was he surprised by Reumah's presence or the mention of her husband's affection? Hannah shook images of the pagan priest's chamber from her memory.

"Going up the mountain will be the most difficult," Mereb stuttered.

Reumah's hand shot up, quieting any more words from Mereb.

Mereb scurried by Naabak's cart without a glance.

"Is my husband ready to be moved?" Reumah rubbed her pimpled skin.

Hannah nodded. "He is ready and eager." Weren't they all eager for an end to this pilgrimage, for an end to Naabak's suffering, and possibly an end to their own suffering, especially if leprosy waited beneath their skin? She desired to be free from her curse, but what if the prophet failed her again? Failed Naabak? Could she accept captivity? Even death?

Reumah let the drape of her mobile chamber fall to the frame. Hannah closed her eyes. If this journey determined her future, she could accept her lot in life. But she could never accept any harm coming to Gil.

"Hannah?" Gil's voice brought her back to the chaos.

He bent low and regarded her as if she were the most beautiful of blossoms. "Let me draw you some water."

Shaking her head, she refused his offer. He had to shoulder Naabak's burden up a steep mountain. Not she.

"The skins need filling. I will drink from the barrel and rest in the shade. You will sweat soon enough, Husband." Oh, what wouldn't she give to make that lie a truth. He had stolen a kiss in the pit and left her wanting more. More kisses, and more of him.

She grabbed an empty goat's bladder slung from the corner of Naabak's cart and cleared her mind of lustful images. She discreetly brushed Gil's hand as Susa pushed his charge forward. "*Shalom*," she whispered.

Hannah turned the stopple on the barrel and began to fill the empty skins. Warm droplets of water trickled down her hand. Every minute they waited to start their ascension, the prophet gained ground. How much time did Naabak really have? His hammock of ram skins would heat with the sun and grow damp with sweat.

The shade from the barrel grew longer.

Her gaze stayed on the mouth of the skin, but she knew who flanked her back. Dread slithered across her shoulders and down her spine. Her fingers trembled. Water cascaded off her hand.

"Did I startle you?" It was not a true question. Too much pleasure rumbled in Konath's voice. "You did not think I would stay behind in the valley, did you? Allow your husband to bash the commander's head in with a rock? And you to flee to your countrymen?"

"It would speed your ascension to the King's right hand." She capped the skin and stood.

"I can wait a few more days until Naabak's body is stiff." His voice lowered. "What will his grieving wife give me for my comfort? Her allegiance? Her body? After all, I stood by her husband to the end."

You wicked vulture. "She will need time to grieve."

"Some. I am discreet."

Hannah clutched the full skin to her chest. "You sicken me."

"Because I spoil your plot to rebel on the mountain and run to safety." His breath was heavy upon her head covering. "You would leave Naabak to rot faster than me. Only, I have to bring his body back to his men."

"What if the prophet heals Naabak? What then?" She braced her hand against the barrel in case she needed to flee.

Konath's laughter did not soar like Gil's but instead sank to the depths of his bowels. "His own god would not heal his disease. Why should your God?"

Her jaw dropped open at his mockery. "Do you not fear your own god?"

"I fear no one but the King of Aram. When he trusts me like a brother, I will have more power than the gods." Konath stretched his arms toward the sky as if challenging Hadad to strike him down. The thunderous god didn't act. Neither did hers.

"You are drunk." What other explanation was there for a man to challenge his own god? She turned to leave.

He cinched her arm, drawing her close. "Not yet. But I will drink when I celebrate my command. And I will celebrate with you."

Bile burned the back of her throat. "I will not leave this land. God has given it to my people. You captured me once. Never again." She glared into his dark eyes and sank into their harsh emptiness.

"Then when Naabak dies, you had better jump from the mountain. For all he has will be mine. And I will not stay in the land of the Jews."

And she and Gil would not leave it.

19

The mountain loomed with deep catacombs and clefts that resembled eye sockets in a skull. The midday sun settled over the mountaintop, blinding all who dared look to the tip of their route.

Konath led the party of prophet seekers with Susa at his side. Naabak's guard had his sword drawn, ready to skewer an enemy at every turn. Gil and Mereb carried Naabak on a hammock of ram skins sewn over poles. Mereb mumbled a low prayer, to whom Hannah did not know. Was it a prayer of protection from Naabak's illness? She would need God's mercy twofold, for her fingers had sunk into the pus on Naabak's skin many times.

Reumah followed behind her husband, remaining somber. She did not pray, but then she had offered her body to Hadad's priest and her husband still suffered.

Pulling a donkey loaded with waterskins and food, Hannah trailed behind everyone. How fast could an elderly prophet travel with two days of lead time? She hoped the man of God ambled slowly, weighed down with whatever brought him to call on God from the cliff tops.

Mereb stumbled.

She gasped and slackened the lead on the donkey. Naabak nearly landed head first on the path.

Reumah shouted for help and slapped Mereb's

shoulder.

"My arms have drained of life," Mereb offered as an excuse.

"He is a shell of himself," Reumah said. "If he was well, you would not be able to lift his leg."

"I shall pour us all a drink." Hannah loosened one of the waterskins. She had thought Naabak would die of leprosy or of the heat, not of being dropped by a servant.

Konath adjusted his braided leather chest shield and glared at Mereb as if he contemplated slicing off the servant's head.

"There is a cave up ahead," Konath said. "Hebrew, search it out."

When no one obeyed Konath's order, she noticed Konath meant her, not Gil. Her mouth parched.

Susa came and stood by the donkey. The soldier did not look amused at his duty.

"Go and see if there is room for the commander," Konath's voice rumbled. If you come across your prophet, do not hesitate to introduce us."

"Call to me if there is movement," Gil said as she passed. The rush of Gil's words made her heart sink to her stomach. He appeared weak and winded.

"I do not fear the prophet." She assured him with a smile. "Only a wild animal."

The depth and the darkness of the cave blinded her more than the sunlight. Blinking to adjust her sight, she listened for a growl, a shuffle, or an unsettled pebble.

Nothing.

The catacomb was not deep, but it was cooler than the trail. A welcome refuge from the heat. She scanned the shadows for life. One corner. Another corner. And anoth—

She spied something slumped against a large rock.

Her knees nearly buckled. She stifled a scream.

Bones. The remains of a man or woman. She did not know which.

Her father's voice rang a priestly warning in her head: *Do not touch the dead. For you do not know how they died.* She moved closer to investigate. This couldn't be the prophet. A body needed more than days to decay to dust.

The skull of the deceased had been struck with something heavy enough to leave a hole. The tunic had fed plenty of rodents. No satchel or purse remained. Not only had life been taken from this person but also its coin.

Backing out of the cave, she stopped short. Konath towered over her.

"Bandits prospered here." She shuddered at the thought that they may still be prowling the mountain. "This hole is a tomb for their victim. I did not see any other life."

"Is it your prophet?" Konath's question held hidden pleasure.

"Only a fool would attack the mouthpiece of God. The body is but bones, so I cannot tell much about this traveler."

"We will rest here then. Bring the water and fruit." Konath's command echoed inside the catacomb.

She waited for Gil and Mereb to lay Naabak on level ground before carrying in the food and drink. Konath inspected the remains. He seemed more concerned with the dead than the living.

"A careless Jew." Konath kicked at the nearest limb.

"How can you be certain it is one of my brothers?" Gil took the cup she offered him. "There are no possessions, no clothing."

"He was dumb enough to get ambushed, was he not?"

Gil stilled. He did not drink. Was he contemplating a fight for the insult? She discreetly touched his back and felt his muscle soften.

"Can we not get rid of that corpse?" Reumah sat on a smooth rock ledge near her husband.

"Even the dead stare at your beauty." Konath's smirk made Hannah relive the night she interrupted his pleasing of her mistress.

Reumah's attention stayed with Naabak.

Konath cocked his head like he expected a gracious response.

Hannah refilled Reumah's cup lest her mistress faint from the heat or Konath's penetrating stare.

"I am parched as these dry bones, slave." The edge to Konath's voice made Hannah replenish his cup in haste.

Konath kicked the dead man's rib cage. His leather-booted foot cracked a bone in half. The sound, like the snap of driftwood, chilled Hannah's blood.

The skull severed from its spine and rolled, resting near Reumah's feet.

Reumah screamed and shifted to keep the decayed head from touching her sandals.

Naabak's body jerked.

Hannah bent low to comfort him and check his sores. Gil prodded the skull with a stick. The gleam in his eyes revealed a desire to whack it back at Konath.

A ribbon of black slithered out of the empty eye socket. In one breath, a poisonous asp struck Reumah's calf and latched on to her skin through her silken skirt.

Shrieks rattled the cave.

Hannah raced toward Reumah. A surge of energy flooded her limbs. Instinctively, she knew what she had to do even before Naabak began rasping orders.

Gil grasped the snake's head and pinched it, freeing the fangs from Reumah's flesh.

Hannah crouched before Reumah. Sweeping aside the garment of her mistress, she swallowed hard, placed her lips around the bite, and sucked. Sucked until her cheeks ached and her belly wretched. Sucked until drool seeped from her mouth. Sucked until a hand at her collar ripped her from Reumah's leg.

She heard Gil's frantic question. "Why?"

20

"Puh," was the only sound she could make as saliva spewed from her mouth. She could not taste the venom but her cheeks tightened like twisted rope. "Puh, puh, puh."

On hands and knees, she drooled like a sick dog. Her mouth drained on its own making a puddle in the dirt.

"What have you done?" Gil reprimanded.

Was saving Reumah's life a sin? She shook his hand off her shoulder. She had to get outside before her stomach erupted.

Covering her mouth, she ran into the sunlight and vomited over the side of a boulder. Collapsing onto the warmth of the large rock, she lay on her belly like a lump of dough waiting to be baked. Her lips pulsed in protest of the poison.

"Is that pagan woman worth your life?" The rebuke in Gil's voice reverberated through her temples.

She closed her eyes. The sun had become too bright. "Reumah," she whispered.

"Mereb is attending to her." His tone softened. "I will get a wet cloth for your mouth."

"No. I might swallow the water. It will cause me more pain."

He gently rolled her on her side. He meant well, but she longed for the security of the rock.

"Your lips are not dark. That is a good sign." It may have been a good sign, but a reprimand rippled through his assessment. He did not seem relieved.

"Are you angry?" She tried to decipher why his face stayed wrinkled like that of an old man. "Reumah could have died."

"So could you have perished." The lines in his forehead softened.

The fight fled from her body. She lay draped as a sheet over a rock on the side of a mountain. Still captured. Still cursed. She looked into Gil's questioning eyes.

"Would that be so bad?" she whispered.

His head bent low. "Is that what you want? To die? To leave me?" His voice rose, sending a skink skittering among the rocks.

It was not her desire to take her own life. God gave life and took it away. But she did not deserve Gil. Why he didn't hate her for all the trouble she had caused him, she did not understand.

"Hannah."

The breath of her name on his lips released a lifetime of hidden shame. Tears dampened her cheeks. She pushed herself from the rock.

"Oh, Gilead." She sat and wiped the wetness from her face, "I am growing weary of all this trouble."

"If you were not here, I would not be in trouble. I would have set myself free. If necessary, by bloodshed."

"You would shed innocent blood?"

"Are they innocent?" The fierceness in his eyes reminded her of a savage predator.

He knew the law as well as she did. He had told her that once. These foreigners mocked God, but had

God condemned them?

"I am not innocent," she said. "I bear the stain from someone as detestable as these foreigners."

"You are a daughter of Aaron and a daughter of Zebula." He took her hand and sat beside her. "The prophet will set you free from your burden."

His surety refreshed her soul. "You are too certain. What if he does not heal me? Or heal Naabak?"

"Then he will have to deal with me." Gil struck his chest.

She smiled weakly but the seriousness of their plight bound her hope.

"There will be no sadness. Not here on our mountain." He emphasized their ownership of this place. She wanted to believe him. Believe that God had a plan. Believe that all her pain would be buried on this rock.

Gil scanned the height of the mountain. He seemed to study every crevice, every alcove. Bathed in the harsh sun, he radiated like an angel. "Where is the life in this mountain? At the end of our harvest, the landowner throws a banquet for his trusted workers. There is a feast. And wine." The celebration blazed in his eyes. "We eat for days, and when we are full, we lay by a stream. A fig tree gives us shade."

She angled toward him, enjoying the anticipation she heard in his voice. Her thoughts did not linger on the food. "I am not one for banquets."

His thumb caressed her knuckle. "I want you to rest in the shade with me. Alone. Just you and me."

When she looked at his eyes, they sparkled with her reflection. In truth, she ached to be his wife. To lie with him. She shuddered at her sinful thoughts. But she did not turn from them. Or from him.

"Will you go there, Hannah?" His voice sounded strangled.

She closed her eyes and tried to picture the running water, the green fronds, the shaded grass.

Opening her eyes, she held his gaze and squeezed his hand. "I will go there." The warmth in his fingers radiated through her hands. She shifted closer. The heat from his body was better than the sun drenched rock.

"With me?"

"Only with you."

He lined her lower lip with his thumb. "Then stay alive with me so we may go there."

She kept her longing in check, but her heart was heavy, full to the brim like a merchant's purse. She wanted to be with him, but they were still in bondage. "I shall do my best."

"There you are, lazy girl," Mereb shouted.

Her heart skipped a much-needed beat.

Gil released her hand.

"What are you doing?" Mereb questioned Gil as if he had a right to an answer.

"I was checking her lips," Gil said. "The venom has worn off."

"Then come inside." Mereb practically pulled her from the rock.

Gil braced an arm against Mereb's chest.

Mereb released his grip on her tunic. "Naabak says I cannot tie a bandage on his wife. No one does it like the girl."

"So that is why he has spared me." She grinned while she stood. Her vision blurred. A whirlpool spun between her ears. Was it the poison? Or the dread of going back into the dark cave?

"Hurry." Mereb waved her inside. "I cannot do your work."

"No one can." Gil placed a supportive arm across her back.

Was she worthy of praise? She had agreed to lie beside a man who was not her husband. Even though he had not mentioned marriage.

21

Reumah's puncture wounds would heal. Even with a bandaged leg, she rallied the caravan to overtake the prophet.

Hannah stumbled and braced herself against the neck of the donkey. The foal brayed. Her toe throbbed from the assault of a jagged rock. Navigating a narrow path while the sun sneaked behind the mountaintops proved painful for her feet.

"We will camp in the width of the bend." Konath's order thundered to the cliff tops.

"I can carry on through the night." Gil motioned to Susa. "Light a torch. The cool air will hasten our steps."

"I give the orders, slave." Konath rounded on Gil. "The women must rest."

Reumah held a vigil beside her husband's body. "I prefer the cover of darkness to the burning sun."

"Why don't we ask your husband or the Jew who took your venom?"

Hannah was not about to bed down for the night. The faster they traveled, the sooner they would catch the prophet, the sooner this perilous journey would end.

"I am fit to go on." She echoed Gil's and Reumah's decision.

Mereb grunted his approval and adjusted his grip on Naabak's bed.

"Shall we continue, Commander?" Konath's question held an air of hubris.

Hannah gripped the donkey's reins and pictured a lash to Konath's cheek. He acted like Naabak's position, Naabak's wife, and Naabak's riches were already his own.

No answer came from the bed.

Reumah gasped. She covered her face with trembling hands.

"Master?" Hannah's voice squeaked like a rusted flute.

No reply came.

She darted to Naabak's side.

Do not leave me. You cannot leave me. Not here. Not when we are so close. You saved my life. Now let my God save yours.

Gil and Mereb laid the skin flat on the ground.

Holding one hand in front of where Naabak's nose had been, she waited for a wisp of breath. Her other hand rested on Naabak's forehead. Fire raged under his skin.

A breath puffed against her fingers. Slight, but there. He was alive. Barely.

She fought the sting of tears behind her eyes. "We must go." Her stare, sharp as a lance, swept from Gil to Reumah to Susa. "The prophet cannot be too far ahead." The haunting chant of an owl agreed with her assessment.

Konath's cackle silenced the bird. "You drag us up a mountain in search of a holy man and now you expect us to march all night."

"We are wasting time." She matched Konath's fervor. "This is what Naabak wanted. We have letters from your King."

"What good are letters without your prophet?" Mereb sided with Konath. "Where is he anyway? Are we to trust a Hebrew seer? It may all be lies."

"You are well versed in lies," she spat back. "Admit your feebleness, you old Moabite."

Mereb sliced the air with his fist and sputtered foreign gibberish.

Konath and Susa laughed. Mereb's indignant huffing caused more raucous laughter.

A fiery rage heated Hannah's skin from foot to head.

"Fine. Laugh." She dismissed them with a flip of her wrist. "You are weaving Naabak's burial clothes." She looked to Reumah for support. Too weary to carry this burden on her own, she needed Naabak's wife to favor the scales.

"Pick up my husband." Reumah pointed at Mereb and then turned toward Konath. "And do not tell me the soldiers of Aram need a rest like nursing babes."

"Of course not." Konath's expression sobered. "We do not nurse at the breast." He thrust Susa forward. "Light a torch and carry on."

"I will serve water," Hannah offered. She feared for Gil's health.

"You do not need to serve me." Gil lifted Naabak with ease. "I am accustomed to the heat in the fields. I am kin to a camel."

Mereb struggled to grip the pole. "I can think of other animals you are kin to," he mumbled.

Hannah walked toward the waiting donkey. "I do not mind." Loosening the waterskin, she sought God's wisdom.

Why do you let us tarry? I have seen your prophet heal a boy with worse disfigurement than Naabak. Have mercy on us. If you need only heal one, then heal my master. Not me. Heal Naabak. If I am not worthy to appeal to you, remember the dedication of my father and my brother.

All through the night, with every carefully placed step on the path, pain radiated through her legs to her knees and down to her feet. When she rested her eyes, the stain of the yellow-orange glow of the torch was all she saw. How much longer could Naabak last?

An eternity later, the sun prowled behind distant mountaintops. Another day of dry winds and cracked lips. The relentless march continued.

Gil's stride shortened. The starvation and beatings had weakened his flesh. But not his determination.

Mereb's sandals scraped the path, leaving a wake for her to follow.

"Halt," Susa yelled. He darted up an embankment.

Her heart beat wildly as if a whip had cracked near Gil's flesh. She dropped the donkey's lead.

At Reumah's urging, Hannah climbed a wall of rocks. She spied a lone tent stitched of blackened skins pitched in a clearing.

Praise be to God!

"Look to an ambush," Konath shouted.

"He is here," she informed the rest of the party. It had to be the prophet. If it was anyone else, she would berate them for being on this mountain.

"Call to him." Gil's voice sounded winded, but he stood tall, his strength appearing renewed by the prophet's presence.

Stepping rock to rock, down into the clearing, onto a surface that appeared to be made by the fist of an angry god, she recalled her meeting with the prophet. Would he remember her affliction? Her lineage? Or punish her for disturbing his solitude? He had not been harsh with her that day. He had not been harsh with her brother for questioning his actions and demanding her healing.

She hesitated to barge into the tent. What if the prophet was in prayer? What if she offended him? What if he refused her request? Again.

Konath scaled the rocks. "Wake him."

The pounding in her chest rose to her throat and fluttered there like a pigeon before a blazing altar. She coughed out the prophet's name. The name she had heard her father speak on the day of her humiliation.

Susa joined her in front of the tent.

The flap vibrated in the breeze.

"Blessed One," she beckoned. "It is Hannah *bat* Zebula."

She swayed as she waited for the prophet to answer. Was he recovering from his travels? Time was not Naabak's ally.

"Forgive my boldness." Her voice strengthened on the last word. "My master is near death." She tried to peek inside the prophet's dwelling.

Konath stomped into the clearing.

"Arise, prophet. We have toiled long enough." Konath whipped the tent flap open.

She gasped at his insult.

A horse hair blanket lay on the ground.

Flat.

Empty.

Was this the house of the prophet or another pilgrim?

Konath seized her arm. Her head flung backward. "Where is your priest? Is this a trick? To plot against me and my men?"

Tremors quaked her arm. "You have my word. He

is here upon the mountain. The men of Mannaseh would not lie."

"Unhand her, you fool." The prophet's voice warbled with indignation.

Hannah turned her head. The prophet, wrapped in a cloak, stood a few feet from Konath. The holy man's hair was damp and his clothes dripped. He wielded his staff like a sword. The wooden rod slammed into Konath's shoulder. No armor spared the collarbone near Konath's neck from the blow. The gut-tightening crack ricocheted through the clearing.

Konath dropped to his knees and howled curses in Aramean.

In awe of the prophet's boldness, she jumped backward, away from Konath's retribution.

The prophet raised his staff as if to take another swipe at Konath or a new swipe at Susa. "Remove your boots of war, heathen. You are defiling the tabernacle of Jehovah."

22

"Remove yourself." The prophet's voice shook. He prodded Konath's chest with the end of his staff like Konath was a rutting boar. The bronze discs on Konath's armor vibrated with each ram of the rod.

"This is your holy one?" Konath grasped at the knotted wood.

Susa came to his commander's side. His hand hovered over his sword.

"Yes," she said forcefully, hoping Konath and Susa would not retaliate against the prophet's assault. An assault brought on by a man who looked different than that day in Jerusalem. The prophet's hair and beard were grayer and longer than she remembered. But in the city, she hadn't interrupted the prophet's private bath. "Step back and give him room." She gestured to where Naabak lay.

Konath and Susa retreated.

The man of God stilled his staff and held it shoulder height. He barred entrance to his tent.

She dropped to her knees in reverence. "Anointed One. We have sought you out for we are in great need. I am a Levite. The daughter of Zebula. Do you remember your servant from Jerusalem?"

The prophet shuffled toward her.

Keeping her face low in the dirt, she prayed the staff would not accost her back. Drops of water dampened the ground in front of her face.

"Arise, daughter."

She stood and beheld the prophet's lofty gaze. It had been weeks since she came before him with her father and brother at her side. She had been the daughter of the chief priest, not the servant of a foreigner.

"You have traveled with the enemies of Israel? These idol worshippers?" His staff quivered as it indicated the group on the path. His chastisement sounded like her father.

"I have—"

"I am no foreigner." Gil bowed briefly. "I am a man of Judah. An escort to this daughter of the tribe of Levi."

She welcomed Gil's presence at her side.

The prophet lowered his staff and squinted at Gil. "You have journeyed far from your people." Doubt echoed in his tone. "What is your tie to this woman?"

She did not meet the prophet's stare. She looked to Gil. His ruddy face had lost its exuberance. They had no blessed bond. No betrothal. Their coupling consisted of hasty words spoken to a wagon master, lustful men, and an enemy commander. The lie had spared their lives.

The sigh from Gil's chest sounded like a storm wind off the Jordan River. "I have no formal ties to this woman."

Reumah gasped. Mutterings began between Mereb and his mistress. Would the prophet have known the truth? Was this a test? She and Gil had traveled to question the prophet's wisdom. Would he dismiss them because of this lie?

"Gilead has taken the place of a kinsman. For my

safety."

"Has he now? Looked out for your innocence as any upstanding relative would?" The prophet moved closer in earnest.

She pushed the image of Gil's kiss in the pit from her mind. Sweat trickled from her head covering down the side of her face. *Woe to me if the prophet knows my thoughts.*

"Yes, Gil...uh...Gilead has accompanied my master as well. Naabak has an urgent need." She indicated the commander. She wanted to avoid questions about Gil. Questions she did not know how to answer. What if Gil brought up her own need of healing before they dealt with Naabak's illness? "My master is sick and dying." She swiped the wetness from her face and pretended to be smoothing her hair.

"Master?" the prophet echoed. "Who is your Master but the God of Israel?"

"No one is greater. Forgive me." Her apology sputtered from her lips.

Konath stomped forward and used Gil's body as a shield from the prophet's rod.

"This girl," Konath said with contempt, "has spirited the commander of the Aramean forces unto this mountain in search of you. She has spoken of your power to heal the sick."

The prophet paced in front of the tent opening. His eyes narrowed. His forehead buckled. The man of God surveyed Konath, his armor, and his weapons.

"I do not act upon my own accord. It is God who chooses to act through me." The prophet gripped his beard with such angst, she thought it might rip free from his chin. "What are my powers as a man?"

"Then call on God to act." Gil threw up his hands

as if he was petitioning the One True God himself. "You refused this woman once. She sought you out. Now, she is in peril. Surely God will take on her burden and spare her a life of disgrace."

"Silence, slave." Konath yanked Gil backward. "We are here for the King's anointed."

Gil lunged at Konath but the prophet's staff separated the two men. The pointed rod caught Gil under the chin. He stepped back, rubbing his neck.

The prophet's head shook from side to side as though he were a parent embarrassed by the conduct of his children. His gray hair, almost dry from the morning heat, obscured his face. "Oh woman," he sighed with a haughty click of his tongue. "Why do you disturb me with a pagan's illness?"

Her mouth parched. She flexed her fingers. Her palms burned from the indentations of her fingernails. How foolish she was to think she could persuade the prophet to rescue Naabak. Rescue Gil. And rescue her. Her heart raced like a shepherd boy running after a prized sheep. *Speak the truth.*

"He saved my life. More than once. He spared me rape at the hands of his men." Shame shivered through her chest and arms, pimpling her skin. "He spared Gilead from a brutal end."

She turned toward Gil. His death would disintegrate her soul. Konath had promised that end if he assumed power over Aram's armies. Desperation emboldened her spirit.

"I saw you grow flesh on a crippled boy's leg. I believe you can heal Naabak. Heal the sores that plague a good man. Even though he is a foreigner. I can accept that it may not be my time. That you have foresight into the future." Her voice rose. "But Naabak does not have time to spare."

The prophet did not speak or call on the name of the Most High God.

Her ears rang with the hum of clashing cymbals. Tears pressed against her eyes. The wind whipped through her bones. She had seen the prophet heal the decayed and the dying. She prayed he would do it here on the mountain, one more time, for Naabak, for Gil. *For me.*

"We have come so far." Her voice squeaked. "We have nowhere to go but here. To you. To our God."

"Show the heathens that the Living God walks with Israel." Gil boasted loudly even though no sword hung on his hip.

The prophet strolled passed his tent. "Come," he said as casually as if she had requested to buy fig cakes at the market. He beckoned her to follow with his staff. "Bring the ill, the foreigners, the man of Judah."

"If he still breathes after this delay," Konath said. "Can you raise the dead?"

"Can Hadad?" Gil challenged.

She hurried to Naabak's side before Konath's rage flared again.

Naabak's eyes beheld her face.

"We have found the prophet." She placed a hand to his head.

"So I've heard." A gurgling sound sputtered from Naabak's chest.

"Be strong husband," Reumah encouraged. "Their high priest has summoned you." A triumphant smile graced Reumah's features. The toil of trudging through the night had vanished.

They followed the prophet around a jut in the mountain and up a trail that widened into another clearing. It appeared part of the mountain had been crushed with a mill stone and storms had blown away the remnants. The prophet halted at a cistern, a small pond bound by walls of smooth rock. The ledge, flat as a widow's purse, tilted inward. Heaven's own funnel.

Water filled the basin. Was it the same water that bathed the prophet?

Gil and Mereb lowered Naabak beside the handmade well.

Konath kicked at the etched stone. "What is this? My Lord does not need a bath."

"It is customary." The prophet said, his attention focused on the sky.

"For purification," Hannah blurted out. She didn't want Konath's anger to pour forth. "There are large vessels outside of the temple for cleansing." She envisioned the stone jars back at the cave, the sheet, Gil's nakedness.

The prophet angled her direction. He couldn't read her mind. Could he?

"Can the foreigner climb inside?" the prophet asked.

She eyed the basin's wall. "The commander has not used his hands or feet in some time. He has neither fingers nor toes." How could Naabak's limbs bear his weight?

"With a man on each side, he can be lowered into the water for cleansing," Gil offered.

The prophet sat on a boulder near the basin. "He will need to dip himself."

"Hah." Konath's head flung backward. His cackle was harsh enough to ripple the water. "This is an insult," Konath yelled. "Can you not wave your palm over him? Recite some Hebrew chant?"

She stiffened. Didn't Konath fear the wrath of that staff?

"The daughter of Zebula and I will go alongside," Gil said. He bent to whisper in her ear. "Dip with Naabak. Perhaps the water will take away your curse."

A hint of a smile crinkled one side of the prophet's mouth. "You are bold, Judah. Was your father a warrior such as these?" His staff jabbed at Konath and Susa.

The men avoided the rod but straightened at the praise.

The intensity of Gil's glare caused her breath to catch in her chest.

"You tell me, man of God." Gil's harsh tone was one she hoped to never hear again.

Naabak grunted. He struggled to sit. The movement distracted Gil. Mereb pushed at the goat skin, propping Naabak's torso against the basin.

"I will dip myself." Naabak moaned and rested a bloody stump on the ledge of stone.

Reumah lowered herself beside her husband. She patted his side where the goat skin still covered his diseased flesh.

Reumah's closeness to her husband's wounds stunned Hannah. Reumah had rarely visited the cave or held a vigil for her husband. She had welcomed Konath to her bed, and in the priest's chamber, she had lounged nude as a newborn. The fire in the rubies on Reumah's rings and bracelets sparkled as she stroked her husband's jaw. The scarlet jewels matched the red sores surrounding Naabak's nose.

The red baubles reminded Hannah of the bracelet she had left for Gil. He had found her because of a gift her father had bestowed on her. A gift to celebrate the healing ceremony. A gift that had summoned Gil into a life of captivity.

"You have always been strong, Husband. What is one swim in this pool?" Reumah's fingers trembled as she drew away from Naabak.

"One," the prophet huffed. He pointed to the basin with his staff. "Not one time. Seven times."

The prophet's proclamation hung in the air like a stubborn cloud. Did Naabak have the strength to support his body in the cistern? How would the water's salts affect the holes in his toes, his hands, his face?

If Naabak drowned, the pool would become a blood bath.

A Hebrew blood bath.

23

"Humiliation." Konath's voice thundered with the power of calling troops to war. "Is Aram to suffer at the feet of Israel? Wash like a dog in a puddle several times over?"

"Trickery," Mereb echoed. "That girl is a spy. The King of Israel sent her to lure Aram into this valley."

Hannah bit down on her lip, dumbstruck by Konath's deceit. He would be the first to hold Naabak under the water so he could assume command of the King's army and stroll into Reumah's bed. Hannah had risked her life and Gil's life to bring Aram's commander to the prophet. All that was required for healing was a washing. A ceremonial cleansing of sorts. Hadn't Jews done this for years?

"Did I not plead for peace?" she said. "Introduce you to our prophet? I am not the merchant of deception." She blinked to clear the blur in her vision.

"You have done nothing but place my men in peril and force me upon this mountain." Konath feigned an interest in the cistern. He leaned closer to her. "Rekindling the hope of my woman is unforgivable. I will exact my revenge slowly on your lover." He sneered at Gil. "You, O Israel, shall watch and be second."

Gil stepped closer to her side. He tensed his muscles. Lines formed on his skin. As always, he was ready to defend or attack. She wished for a time when the fighting would end and she and her protector could be a simple man and woman on the streets of Jerusalem. She prayed her father had not made arrangements with Azor. Even as her feet skimmed this sacred ground, she longed to be with Gil and lie by his side.

"It is a simple task for a seasoned warrior to dip in the pool." Gil backed his way toward Naabak, his eyes constantly assessing the closeness of Konath and Susa. "A wise soldier would heed the prophet."

She helped Gil raise Naabak. Reumah scolded Mereb for his laziness.

"Go," Gil whispered in her ear. "Ask the prophet if you can dip with Naabak." He urged her onward, excitement sparking in his eyes.

Hannah turned toward the prophet. The old man's eyes drooped. He pitched forward as if he would tumble off the boulder he sat on. *Can he not stay awake with us?*

Lightly, she tapped his shoulder. The prophet's eyes beheld her as a misbehaving child.

"Why not a prayer over Naabak or a touch of his flesh? I know this healing can be done with ease. I have seen it with my own eyes."

The prophet's face was unmoved like the rock that held his weight.

Her lungs cinched for having woken the prophet, but she remembered her father saying that once water is drawn from the well, it may as well be poured. She was determined to dump the pitcher. Naabak clung to the ledge of the pool. Her curse clung to her soul.

"And what is to become of me? Will I someday be a clean woman?" Her voice warbled.

The prophet flailed his hand and cast her off like a gnat. He stood and hobbled toward the clearing where his tent was staked. "There is a time for everything."

Her mouth fell open. "You are leaving us? Here? Now?" Her voice sputtered.

"I am no stranger to Jerusalem. I will see you again. And your commander has men to attend to him. For now, I must rest."

She watched him leave, her feet heavy as millstones, her body as empty as a wineskin after a week-long wedding. She was still unclean. Still cursed. Still held captive. Her fists hammered at the heavens.

A boisterous laugh caught her attention.

Gil shouted, "Three."

She ran toward the basin. Rounding a corner, she skidded to a stop. Susa blocked the trail.

"Your holy man is tired?" Disbelief tainted Susa's voice.

Is that all Susa had heard? Had he heard of her curse? He did not pull away from her, frightened by God's outcast. She dutifully dipped her head. "It is customary for him to rest and pray."

Susa chuckled and let her pass.

When she entered the clearing, Naabak clung to the edge of the pool. Water spurted from his nostrils, hissing like water sprayed on hot coals.

"They are making a fool of you," Konath shouted. "Will you not drown before you finish this mockery?"

Blasphemer! How dare that seducer insult her God?

Hannah raced toward the cistern to help Gil. No daughter of a Levite priest was going to be enslaved any longer on holy ground.

24

"Four," Gil counted, bending and gripping Naabak's wrist.

Hannah scanned the man-made well. She didn't want Gil to find out its depths by retrieving Naabak's corpse.

Naabak surfaced. His body shook like a vibrating tambourine. Flesh peeled from his face.

"Give up this farce," Konath instructed. He battered the ledge of the basin with his leather boot. "What salve does this cistern hold? Were your sores not washed in Aram? You will drown. Then who will heal you? That old man?"

Reumah trembled. Sitting next to the stone wall, she rested her head on her knees and hid her face like a chastised child.

Gil glared at Konath. Turning his back on the naysayer, he said, "Breathe. Now." His voice was as calm as if he was keeping order in the gleaning fields. "Three more."

Her master did not submerge his head, his shoulders, or his chest. Was he giving up? Doubting the prophet? She shivered even though sun drenched the clearing, searing every edge of chiseled rock. Naabak could not give up.

Hannah removed a bandage from her belt. "This is

not for sport." She stood by Gil, forming a wall of encouragement. "Nor folly." She reached out to Naabak and offered him the cloth to cover his nose.

Naabak shook his matted hair. "My burden." He rasped out water and blood. He slipped under the sapphire slate of water.

She took up Gil's count. "Two more," she said as Naabak resurfaced.

"And then it will be your turn." Gil's eyebrows rose, expecting her to agree.

Her heart labored against her rib cage. The prophet had not given her any new revelation. He had not told her to dip in the pool. No mention was made of freedom from her ancestor's sin.

Gil eyed her over his shoulder.

"You are losing count," she teased, not wanting Gil to search out the prophet.

Konath stomped closer. "Our commander will have no strength left to return to his men. Where is the new flesh?" Konath's fingers tapped the hilt of his sword. He drummed his fingernails in an antsy rhythm as if the bronzed blade craved revenge.

Mereb handed Reumah a raisin cake. "Be done with this nonsense."

Reumah pushed the sweet cake away. She crawled nearer her husband and sat sideways on the ledge. "Finish this," she said to her husband. "Do as their advisor says."

Reumah's support of her husband made Hannah cheer her master all the more.

Gil called out, "Seven."

Naabak twisted free from Gil's grasp. He sunk, flailing his stumped hands to keep his bones from crashing to the bottom of the pit.

Hannah stretched over the edge of the basin to glimpse the water's surface. She tried to calm her breaths but they came out in pants of anticipation. Everyone hovered over the pool. A forest of bodies shaded the cream-colored stone.

Bubbles appeared, popping instantly at the water's surface. They stopped.

"Is he drowning? Or dead?" Konath retreated from the basin.

"No. It is not so." The denial sprang from her lips. She needed Naabak alive. Living and whole to spare Gil's life. To give her complete faith in the prophet. To give her complete faith in God.

She thrust her arm into the water, and knocked Gil out of the way. "You cannot leave me." She dug in the water like it was wet river sand.

A hand shackled her wrist and pulled against her weight.

She would not go down. *Lift.* Rearing back, her calf muscles tightened. *Lift.* Gil cinched his arms around her waist. She braced her other hand on the rocks for leverage. She and Gil pulled together as one.

Susa ran to their aid. "What can I do?"

Konath sheltered Reumah from the commotion. "Evil spirits are at work."

Naabak released her wrist. She clawed to hold him anew. Her hand treaded water. "Hear, O Israel…"

Instantly, Naabak shot out of the water like a spawning fish, showering her face with cool droplets. Her master's face was whole, healthy, handsome. Fingers, not rotting flesh, slapped the ledge of the basin.

"Hallelujah," she shouted as Gil flung her around in celebration.

Susa fell to his knees. "Praise be to your God."

Reumah cried out in Aramean. Sobbing, she reached toward her husband.

Konath stumbled backward. His face was pale, his jaw slack.

Naabak lifted himself out of the water. His arms bulged with strength. His feet slapped stone.

He had toes and sinewy legs. He had thick thighs. He had —

Gil's hand covered her eyes. "That's enough gazing," he said, his voice uneasy. "Mereb, get your master a garment."

Mereb tossed a tunic over Naabak's bountiful shoulders and covered his loins.

Naabak had been restored. The God of Israel had answered her prayer. Could a healing of her own be far behind? She clasped her hands over her face and wiped the tears from her cheeks. God was near. God was here.

"God is good," she sang. "*Selah*."

Hannah stared at a miracle. The commander of Aram's army had been wasting away in a hammock of hides and now he embraced his wife forcibly, with passion. She had never seen two people kiss other than in a customary greeting. Naabak and Reumah's kiss lasted and lingered. Gil did not shield her eyes from their desire. Her belly warmed knowing that the heir Reumah desired could come to pass. Joyous laughter jiggled Reumah's chest.

"You."

Her head jerked toward the shout.

The scrape of iron against metal chilled her teeth.

Konath's blade stood ready to strike. Rage, not love or loyalty, quaked the bronze rounds on Konath's breastplate.

She stepped backward into the wall of the basin and lost her balance. Gil grasped her shoulder and shoved her nearer to Naabak. She fell from the force of the push.

Konath's sword gleamed in the vicious sun. He aimed the tip at her heart. "I should have killed you in that stable."

Naabak boomed a command in Aramean.

Konath lunged in her direction with his weapon extended. The jab of the sword came swift.

Her vision blurred. She scrambled to her feet and tried to scream, to draw a defender, but all that came forth was a high-pitched whine.

Gil vaulted in front of her, blocking the sun.

"Run," she cried. Her throat burned, but she had to save Gil.

A dull slicing sound split the air. Her body shook. She knew the sound. Oh, the strange sound of knife on flesh. Of her father and brother butchering livestock in the temple. Of Konath's sword impaling her love. Her stomach heaved.

Oh God, no!

The tip of Konath's blade protruded from Gil's back. Gil pitched forward, slumping over the length of the sword.

"Han—" He never finished her name.

Shrill wails wracked her body. She couldn't stop them. She didn't know how.

The blade rotated and retreated. Blood seeped from the wound. Blood splattered the air, her tunic, her face. Blood. More blood. Gil's precious blood.

"Gi...Gil...lead." Her words stuttered as she wrapped an arm around his waist.

A gurgle reached her ears. Gil stared straight ahead, his eyes hollow and haunting.

Konath had taken her Gil from her.

Along with her future.

25

Gil slumped to his knees, teetering as if the slightest breeze could topple him.

This couldn't be happening. Was it a warning, a vision, a test? Not murder on holy ground. An eerie hum like a swarm of locusts buzzed in her ears.

She dropped to her knees beside Gil. Ripping off her head covering, she pressed the cloth against his belly. Her hand dampened and turned scarlet with the rising swell of blood.

Gil grasped her hand, anchoring her at his side.

"We will get the prophet," she said.

His words broke into pieces, unrecognizable whispers.

She tried to lower Gil to the ground gently, but the weight of his body pulled her over. "Do not leave me," she urged. "The prophet is near."

A shadow fell over Gil's face.

Konath's laugh sent a shudder through her spine. "That slave was a fool to think he could spare you."

"The girl is my servant," Reumah said, hysterics raising her pitch. "A gift."

"Sheath your weapon," Naabak ordered.

Hannah squinted up at Gil's murderer. Her frame shook. "God curse you, you worthless pagan." The threat of Konath's weapon did not deter her condemnation. "How dare you kill one of God's own?"

Konath's sword rose higher.

Her shoulders flinched, but she remained defiant. "You are a foul stench."

"Halt." Naabak unsheathed Susa's sword. He sprang toward Konath, his diseased flesh a distant nightmare. He moved with the strength of a bear and the grace of a skilled swordsman.

She braced for a clank of blades.

Konath's eyes bore down on her but only for a moment.

Polished bronze flashed across his neck.

A wild victory-grin froze on his face as his head was severed from his body.

The *thunk* of Konath's skull upon the unforgiving ground marred the silence.

Her stomach rallied for another emptying.

Gil's hold on her hand slipped away.

"Gil," she beckoned. "Gil." He did not answer. She patted his cheeks. He did not respond. His eyes closed, shutting her out.

She turned to Naabak. "Master, I beg of you. Seek the prophet." Tears flooded her cheeks like storm rains flooded the Jordan.

"It is done, Hannah." Naabak said her name as soft as her mother at bedtime.

"I know." She cradled Gil in her arms. "The prophet of God will pronounce you clean. You can return to Aram. Then he can heal Gil." She pressed her nose to Gil's rough, unshaven jaw. He was still warm. A curl of his hair tickled her nostrils. If only she could breathe in his scent.

Reumah clung to her husband and wept.

Naabak reached out and tugged at Hannah's shoulder. "Israel, he is no more."

What was Naabak babbling about? Had he not received a miracle of God? "The prophet can restore his breath." Her mumbled words lost their force.

"Gil," she whispered. Framing his cheekbones in her hands, she shrieked his name. Her fingers trembled. The ground beneath her seemed to quake.

No laughter rang out. No tease. No taunt.

"Does your prophet heal the dead?" Naabak asked, his tone soft, yet serious.

Stunned, she stared at Naabak, tears veiling her vision. "The prophet healed your skin. He will mend Gilead's." She looked to Gil. He couldn't be gone. He was her escort. They had started this journey together. Together they were supposed to finish it. He would not leave her here on this jagged mountain.

Wrapping her fingers in his lush curls, she bent over his body. The warmth of his skin gave her comfort.

"You promised to take me to your banquet. To lay in the shade side by side. You have never lied to me." Her lungs gulped for air. "You cannot begin now. Not now. Not ever."

Drips of water assaulted her skin, crawling over the back of her arms and neck like worms slithering over the dewed ground. Naabak's hair splattered her again and again as he rocked her gently, trying to break her hold on Gil. His hair, like sopping yarn, rested against her skin. She would not let go, not now, not until the prophet came to save Gil.

The stomp of footsteps rallied a hope inside her heart. Had the prophet come at last? The Blessed One had restored a foreign commander, yet how much more would it take to heal a man of Judah born on Promised Land.

"The tent is empty," Susa reported, his voice filled with disbelief.

Surely the prophet did not leave. Her sobs joined with Naabak's droplets, wetting Gil's face. This wasn't supposed to be--Naabak standing solid and strong while Gil lay lifeless, his blood muddying the dust of Mahanaim.

"Let us take the body to him," Naabak offered.

She shook her head defiantly.

"His lifeblood was spilled by this pool. This place renewed your flesh. Do not take him from this spot, from here, from me. We must wait. The prophet will come for him. He is a Hebrew. A man of Judah." *My man of Judah.*

She sat by the pool and waited, Gil cradled in her arms. Naabak comforted his wife as Susa and Mereb removed Konath's remains. Even with the sun overhead, and the caress of her hands, Gil's body could not hold warmth.

She settled on top of Gil matching him hand to hand, arm to arm, chest to chest, leg to leg. Her feet met his calves. "He has a mother," she said, catching her breath. "He takes care of her." Remembering the pride in Gil's mother's eyes caused her chest to collapse in grief.

"She has gone mad," Mereb declared in his head-of-household tone.

A hand patted her back. "Israel, let us wrap his body before the cold sets in. The prophet has not come."

Turning her head to the side, she saw Reumah, Susa, and Mereb standing in an awkward line, watching the Lord of the Aramean armies comfort a servant girl.

"I am cursed," she said glancing at Naabak. "Cursed from birth. Why do I live and Gil not? As a punishment?" Looking skyward, she called out, "Punish me, Jehovah. Not Gilead."

A cackle of a breath left her lungs. What would her father say if he heard her challenge God? But why had God sent her Gilead and then taken him away? Why save a heathen and let a Hebrew die?

"Did Gil not follow your laws, Jehovah?" she shouted, lifting her chin to the sun. "Did he not love you with his soul?"

Pressing her lips firmly to Gil's, she murmured, "How do I say *Shalom* to you?" She nestled her cheek into the crook of Gil's neck. "Hear O Israel, the Lord is our God, the Lord is One. And you Gilead of Judah, you and I are one."

"Come to me, Hannah." Reumah beckoned with outstretched arms. "Perhaps, Mereb can find some honey to soothe your stomach."

She gazed upon Gil until her heart was too large for her body.

Naabak knelt beside Gil. A few wayward drips from his hair trickled down Gil's skin. "Let us clean the blood from you. The prophet will return to this place. I am certain."

The stained and soaked cloth she wore clung to her body. How many commandments had she broken bathing in blood and touching a corpse? She didn't care. The Law was useless to her. Gil was dead. Inside, she felt as if her lifeblood had drained into the dirt.

It should have been me, Gil. Licking her lips, she kissed him hard and sweet and with spirit, for it would be the last time. When she lifted her mouth, sorrow weighed her down like an anvil. *They want me to leave you now.* But how could she? He had given her everything, and what had she given him in return? His ruin.

She lifted her chest.

A puff of air bathed her nose.

Had Naabak pressed down on Gil's body? Had she?

She rolled off of Gil.

His arm twitched.

Was it a trick of the eyes? Was it because she moved?

Gil's body began to jerk and shiver like it was demon possessed.

"Naabak," she gasped, "what is happening?" Surely in all his battles he had seen the slain settling into death.

Naabak pointed at Susa. "Find the prophet. Hurry."

Gil's forehead creased. His lips pursed into a thin line of pain.

"Oh, God, what is happening?" Tremors wracked her body. Was God pronouncing judgment? "Gil," she rasped, her mouth dry as dust.

Gil's eyes flew open. His gaze found her.

She wailed like a widow. Was this demon possession? Another miracle? Was God himself going to speak?

Naabak wrapped his arms around her and tried to draw her away from the corpse.

And then she saw it. She saw it in Gilead's eyes.

The mischievous moonlight she loved.

26

Gil's brows furrowed as he scanned his surroundings. She tried to say his name, but her voice vanished like it had been snatched by a ghost. She swept tears from her eyes. New tears. Not tears of bitter mourning. Tears of joy.

Struggling to rise to his elbows, Gil slumped to the ground.

"Bring him figs, roasted grain," she shouted at Mereb, her voice squeaking like a worn wheel.

Reumah fell to her knees. "Truly this is a mountain of the gods."

Gil's gaze swept to Naabak. "You are fit, Commander." His hand rose then fell away. "A beautiful woman weeps at my side. Did we celebrate with too much wine?"

Naabak crouched next to Gil. He grasped the hand that held him aloft in the pool. "Konath impaled you on his sword. It is a miracle of your God that you live."

"And you live," Gil mumbled, taking a cake from Mereb.

Hannah began to lift Gil's tunic. "I could not stop the blood. Is the wound healed?"

Gil grasped her arm. "I do not believe I'm bound under my tunic." She could have sworn he tried to laugh at her folly. "I dreamed my bowels were on fire. I called for water but there was not enough to relieve the torment." He tapped his stomach and struggled to sit. "There is no burning or pain. Did you pray for me, Hannah?"

Happiness and pride pulsed through her body. Her words rushed out. "I tended to the blood with a rag and rebuked our God."

Mereb placed a bowl of grain next to Gil. "She smothered your bones and squeezed your blood from your wound."

"I can see that." Gil's eyes narrowed as he took in her blood-drenched tunic.

"I called out to the Lord," she said, chastising Mereb and trying to explain her boldness. "I pled for your life. Our God had spared a foreigner's life, why not one of his own?"

"You are a blessed woman, daughter of Zebula," Naabak said. "I would not have thought as much when you hid in my tent." Naabak turned toward Mereb. "And you. Do not invoke the wrath of a woman. We shall not test her God a third time to raise you, Moabite."

Laughter erupted, but she heard nothing after the commander of Aram proclaimed her blessed. Her curse remained. But Gil was alive. God had heard her prayer. Wasn't Gil's life worth more than her healing? She had lived seventeen years without licking salt or breathing in blossoms. She could live a hundred more knowing that her love lived.

"You do not laugh, Hannah." Gil offered her a bite of his fig cake.

"I will need a dozen fig cakes to take away my weariness."

"Or a pomegranate." His reminder made her chuckle.

She stroked his hand, oblivious to the dried blood. "Repent!"

Everyone turned toward the shout.

The prophet stood, staff extended, jabbing his whittled branch at their celebration. "Repent, you defiler of this nation."

Hannah sat tall. How could the prophet chastise Naabak for killing Konath? The commander spared her life. He avenged Gil's blood.

The staff raised and pointed in her direction. The smooth end of the rod stopped inches from her nose.

"You harlot!"

27

"What?" She crawled backward. Warmth like fire flushed her skin. The prophet knew of her family's reputation. Knew of her innocence. She had knelt in his presence. Prayed at his feet.

"I have not known a man," she said, aghast at his insult.

"Did you not lay on this one?" The prophet pointed his staff at Gil. "Did you not lay your lips on his?" He accused her with his rod, poking it in her direction. Poke. Poke. Poke.

His proclamation hummed in her ears. She was not a prostitute, but she could not deny that she had fallen prostrate onto Gil and kissed his mouth. A farewell kiss.

It was not an untruth. The prophet's stare condemned her. It couldn't be. Was she not only cursed, but sullied?

The prophet lowered his staff and shook his head in judgment.

"I did not touch this man for pleasure." She looked from Naabak to Reumah to Susa to Mereb for affirmation. "Or for lust." At least not this day.

The man of God tilted his chin skyward. His gaze rose above his long nose.

Did he know what she was thinking? She jumped to her feet. Where had the prophet been? She had cared for a fallen Hebrew. Alone. Pointing a finger back at the prophet, she said, "If you had been here, the matter would have been settled. You could have healed Gil with a touch. Susa went in search of you. You had wandered off, leaving me here with enemies of Israel."

Susa squared his shoulders. "I did a thorough scouting."

The holy man remained silent.

Did he want her to repent of all her failings since leaving Jerusalem? Surely, entering the temple of a pagan god required more chastising and atonement than trying to save the dying?

"I am not brazen," she stuttered, trying to calm her ragged breaths. "I called out to God. Whether it was my plea to Jehovah or this place...I do not know. I covered him, mourned for him, and yes, I laid on him." Her posture buckled under the weight of her confession.

Gil stood beside her. She needed him to say what she did was not immoral. She needed his warmth, his laugh, his acceptance.

"So it is true." Gil's voice lowered. "You touched me?" He stroked his jaw as if trying to remember what happened. "Everywhere?"

She nodded and choked back blame. Tears stung her lids but she would not let them fall. Comforting a dying man was not a sin. Not a man who had risked his life to see her healed. Her heart was pure. She wasn't a filthy harlot. When the panic of losing Gil settled upon her, she did what any loved one would do. She bid farewell to his body. And she would do it again.

"Let Aram take the blame," Naabak said, stepping forward in the splendor of ornate armor. "Your God showed me mercy. My soldier ignored a command and acted dishonorably. I came here because of the testimony of this girl. Lay the consequences at my feet."

"No, Master."

Naabak turned at her voice.

"I am unclean. Touching the dead is forbidden. His blood was on my skin. My farewell kiss was more than a ritual. In truth, I did not want the kiss to be the last." Her confession floated in the air. Everyone heard it, but her words were meant for Gil.

Standing on the mountain, her confession echoing above its catacombs, she remembered seeking Gil among the alleys of Jerusalem. Should she repent of her actions, of going into the wilderness with a man she barely knew? Her throat felt like it housed a rock. No. She would never say that her time with Gil was immoral. Spending hours with Gil had been a blessing.

"I sought you out, Blessed One, because I wanted to be healed. You once told me it was not my time. I left Jerusalem to seek when my time would come, or if it already had. Now, I only want to return home." The pinch in her throat made it difficult to continue. "I can live in disgrace. I already have."

"There has to be something we can do?" Reumah addressed her husband and the prophet at a healthy distance. "We have riches. We can make an offering. Pay a sum."

"I have no ties to Gil," Hannah said to her mistress. "He is not my husband." She looked at Gil. "I should have righted all the lies. Even the one on the cart when you addressed me as your wife. I should have stayed in my father's house and accepted my fate."

"Stop." The sharp, angry tone of Gil's voice startled her. He pointed at the prophet, then to Naabak. "This man was sick with fever. He had pus for blood. I had a blade in my back." Gil's hand flayed in the air like he directed music. "Look at us now. We are here and whole only at Hannah's urging. Surely, God has not shunned her. He did not shun any of us."

Gil grabbed her wrist and lifted it high. "Bind us together. I don't remember this woman's body on mine, but I want to."

Hannah's mouth fell open as Gil announced his lust.

The prophet perked up at Gil's proclamation. He stamped his staff as if he was disgusted by the day's events.

Gil squeezed her hand. His touch made her float on a breeze. "I am a lawful man who desires a wife. I have testified that Hannah is my wife. Make it so. Make my falsehood truth."

Her pulse pounded in her temples. She wanted to be Gil's wife. She wanted to be wrapped in his arms from dusk until daybreak. She wanted...him. She hoped her marriage bed thoughts were not gleaming in her eyes.

The prophet shook his head. "Her father is not here to pledge her to you?"

"The girl belongs to my wife," Naabak said, indicating Reumah. "She has been under my protection and in my household." Naabak smiled broadly as though he had conquered a formidable foe. "I give this woman to this man."

"You are not a Hebrew," the prophet scoffed.

"The God of Israel, your god," Naabak emphasized, "restored my body and my command. He brought these two together long before we crossed trails."

"Gilead," the prophet called out, his eyes still resting on Naabak. "Your kinsmen reside in Jerusalem."

"Yes. My mother is the daughter of Abiathar. They await my return." Gil squeezed her hand tighter.

"And your father?" the prophet asked.

"I do not know my father." Gil's voice lowered to a reverent growl.

"Did your mother know him?"

Gil's foot scraped the ground as a ram ready to charge. "No. She did not know the beast." Gil's grip relaxed.

"And you, daughter of Aaron, daughter of Zebula, a Levite." The prophet stomped his rod as he recited her heritage. "If you marry this man from the tribe of Judah, you forfeit the choice meats your father and brother bring from the temple. Will you leave the table of Zebula? Of Shimron?"

Gil let go of her hand and stepped toward the pool. Her hand tingled as it hung by her side. Gil sat on the stone ledge, his hands clasped in his lap. Was he still weak from the impalement?

"What is food to me?" she said. "My dead mouth already keeps me from the table. To me, even the choice meats offered to the priests taste of nothing."

The prophet made an annoying clicking noise with his tongue. If that was supposed to sway her thinking, he had better try something more spectacular. Her nerves had become bold after weeks in Aram.

"By birthright you have been chosen to eat the fatty portions of meat. Your father has been chosen to receive them. Would you cut yourself off from the blessings of your lineage?" She heard the "for him" even though the prophet did not speak it forthright.

"And what blessing would that be?" She clamped her jaw so tight she thought she might break a tooth. "The scorn of my brother? The tears of my mother? The punishment for a sin I did not commit? My father is a proud man, but I do not believe he is proud of me."

"Are you proud of him?" Gil sounded as serious as she had ever heard him.

She didn't know how to answer. Her father had tried to find a cure for her curse. He made offerings in the temple and gained an audience with the prophet. But even he had grown weary and welcomed Azor's bid. She glanced at the prophet. His forward lean made him look anxious for her answer. She whispered, "Yes," for all the years her father had given her hope.

"I am not proud of my father." Gil's confession caused her to turn around. "He left my mother in stalks of wheat, abused and afraid. I cannot offer you a lineage like your father's."

Shame would not cast its lot over her again. She sat on the stone beside Gil and stroked his beard firmly, bringing his gaze upon her. "You accepted me that first day in your"—she lowered her voice so only Gil could hear her—"bedroom." She resumed her normal volume. "You accompanied me to Mahanaim. You fought for me in the olive grove. Saved me in the pit. Our journey is not over."

"You will regret this Hannah *bat* Zebula."

Did he truly believe that lie? Her heart raced. "I have met your mother and seen the love she has for you. That love has grown in me. You are an honorable man fending for the poor and the widows. I have lost you twice as you fended for me. I feared you dead in the grove and when you spared my life on this rock. You had better not leave me again Gilead *ben* Abiathar."

His gaze grew serious as she spoke of her devotion. He cradled her face as if he held a delicate alabaster jar. His thumb was a gentle breeze upon her cheek. "I will not leave you."

"Enough." The prophet's interruption sent a shudder down her back. "Let me be done with all of you." With the crook of his staff, he indicated that she and Gil come forward.

She latched onto Gil's arm as they approached God's spokesman.

The prophet whipped off his belt and wrapped it around Gil's wrist, then hers. Frayed camel's hair pricked her skin.

Naabak, Reumah, and Susa crowded the prophet. Mereb peered over her shoulder.

"Commander of Aram," the prophet began, "do you give this woman of your household to this Hebrew?"

"By my word," Naabak said.

Pulling the belt tight, the prophet continued, "You are joined this day as husband and wife. A bond only God can sever. Gilead, man of Judah, return to your kin with your wife."

Hannah could have sworn she heard the prophet breathe "*Selah*" in praise of their leaving the mountain, but she paid him no heed. Her heart rejoiced. It soared to the clouds. She envisioned dancing all the way to Mahanaim, her feet as wild as the wind.

Nodding to the small crowd, the prophet removed the belt, first from her wrist and then from Gil's. "I am done," the prophet announced. He hiked the rocky path to where his tent was staked.

A smile as big as the Holy Land eclipsed Gil's face. He grasped her wrist and stroked the red ring left from their binding. Her heart spasmed with every slide of his fingers.

"We must celebrate," Naabak said, raising a fist skyward. "Mereb, unfasten the wineskin."

Mereb grumbled at his chore. "You do realize, Mistress, you are down not one, but two servants."

"There are others." Reumah sat at her husband's side. "We will need room for all our children and grandchildren." She beamed at Naabak.

Hannah's stomach flipped at the mention of babies. She would be alone with her husband tonight and she was a clueless virgin.

"Speaking of children," Gil cleared his throat. "Hannah and I will need to bathe. We are unclean."

"Considerably," Mereb quipped before tasting the wine.

Naabak held out his cup. "The pool is all yours. I do not wish for another dip. There are fine linens on the donkeys. Your prophet has refused payment for my healing."

Mereb handed Gil some wine.

Gil tipped the rim of his cup until it clanked hers. "You may peek behind the sheet this night." His grin struck a spark within her chest.

Before she could defend the slip of her hand in the cave, or her curiosity, he leaned forward. "I intend to look my fill."

28

Hannah clung to the ledge of the pool. She couldn't stop the fleeting thoughts of an end to the curse she had carried all of her life. She shook her head and brushed away the idea. How much more could she ask of God? She had been blessed with Gil and his miraculous return to life. She would gladly carry her curse until her bones were dust, simply to be with Gil and share his love.

She let go of the rocks and dipped below the water. She dipped seven times, but not for restoration. She bathed to be clean for her wedding night with her new husband. A shiver of delight tingled across her skin as she envisioned their union.

"This one favors your coloring." Reumah held out an indigo gown.

Blinking to clear the drops of water on her lashes, Hannah admired the weave of golden thread through the dark blue linen. The dress was fit for a princess, not an innocent going to her marriage bed.

"I am accustomed to plain linens." Hannah emerged from the basin and stood on the smoothed stones. She grabbed a sheet warmed by the sun and wrapped her nakedness.

"Not today," Reumah said. "You are a bride given by my husband and you deserve the best. If not for your urging, Naabak would have died in Aram, his line cut off from this life."

"It is a new beginning for you and Naabak." She wrung the dampness from her hair. "I have taken you away from his attentions."

Reumah giggled. "I have received my husband's attentions, and I plan to receive them again tonight." She rubbed her belly as if she were already expecting a child.

Hannah's cheeks warmed. Never had her mother spoken of her father in such a brazen manner.

Reumah's eyes gleamed like a young girl receiving her first gold ring. "That pool has given him the strength and hunger of a young bull."

Hannah forced a smile and a wisp of a laugh at Reumah's revelation as if the talk was commonplace in a priest's household. Sweat dampened her palms. Did her ignorance show? Should she ask Reumah to reveal what was to come this evening when she and Gil were alone? Her mother had no reason to discuss a union with a man. There had been no official betrothal. She shook thoughts of Azor from her mind.

"What is wrong?" Reumah slipped the gown over Hannah's head.

"Nothing." Hannah shivered. The exquisite weave brushed her body, silken and smooth like a flower petal. She wondered what she would do when Gil lifted the linen to her thighs.

Reumah began to braid Hannah's hair. The tingle on her scalp made her bones as light as a bird's. Would Gil's touch make her soar as high?

"Have you known Gilead?" Reumah asked.

Hannah snapped out of her daydream. "Not long." She tilted her head into Reumah's pull.

Reumah's hands stilled. "That is not what I mean."

Reumah's lilting voice ended on a provocative note.

"Oh. No." She turned to view her mistress. "I have never been with a man, though someday I hope to be with child." She tucked a wisp of hair into a tight braid. "It is my dream to be a mother."

"That is a dream we both share." Reumah tied off Hannah's hair with ribbon. If only there were ribbons to hide her ear nubs. Reumah stood and walked to a pile of folded linens.

The weight of the braid rested against Hannah's back. The weight of being a wife rested on her shoulders.

Reumah held up a mustard-yellow head covering. "This will accent the gold thread in your gown. We will secure the cloth with these." She held sapphire-laden gold bands. The blue jewels glistened in the waning sunlight, reminding Hannah of the healing water of the pool.

"I cannot accept such a gift." Hannah feared the gold and gems had come from the villages of Israel, ripped from the dead by Aram's raiders. Had the gold been offered to pagan gods for victory at the expense of her people?

Reumah's smooth fingers cupped Hannah's chin. "You cannot refuse a gift from the commander of Aram's armies. It would be an insult." Reumah's eyebrows rose, daring Hannah to persist in her defiance.

Did she dare persist? She and Gil were still at the mercy of Naabak and Susa's swords.

Reumah released her grasp and flipped the golden head covering over Hannah's braids. "I have my husband and a chance at an heir. My standing has returned twofold because of your faith in the prophet."

Finally, her deformity was covered. Her stomach swirled. Would Gil touch them tonight?

She traced the gold bands on her forehead. Her fingertips rose and fell in the facets of the stones. "I will wear these in remembrance of my time in your household."

"As you should. They were forged in Damascus. These trinkets"—Reumah's breath hitched—"are nothing compared to the jewels that await me now. My father is a harsh man. He was cruel to me when I was your age. The beatings stopped when Naabak sought me to be his wife. To have returned to my father's house a widow without coin or child would have been unthinkable."

Hannah cringed at the thought of what her father and brother would do when they found out she was married. Given in hand by a foreigner to a Hebrew outside of the tribe of Levi.

"Then I am doubly grateful to Naabak for sparing my life, for it has spared yours. Because of Mereb's tricks, I was beaten by Konath. I do not wish those wounds on anyone."

Reumah smiled through tears.

"You are a brave woman, Mistress, for believing in my God."

Sitting beside her, Reumah took hold of Hannah's wrist. "I sensed a truthfulness in you. A spirit I once held. But that is talk of the past. We are not finished here. Your arms are bare."

Reumah layered bracelets of gemstones to Hannah's elbows. One after another they fell, adorning her like a queen. She knew it would be useless to refuse her mistress. The tiny amber flames in Reumah's eyes sparkled brighter than all the riches adorning

Hannah's wrists.

"These gifts are beautiful. I will not take them off." Hannah admired the bright jewels along her arm.

"Oh yes you will. You will take them off or we will hear the music of clinking baubles all night." Reumah giggled.

What could she and Gil possibly do all night? When Hannah's mouth fell open, Reumah laughed all the harder.

Hannah followed Reumah to where they had first glimpsed the prophet's tent. No matter how many times she wetted her lips, they dried like sheets in the searing sunlight. The evening breeze had banished the sun behind the cliffs. Carefully, she plotted each footfall of her newly-gifted sandals. Anxiety strummed her heart as if plucking a harp for pleasure.

Flames from a fire pit illuminated Gil and Naabak. Seeing them standing together conversing in the tongue for trade, warmed her blood more than the thought of a newborn babe. The peaks of two additional tents pointed to the heavens.

Gil glanced up as she and Reumah approached. "The night has begun, Wife." He extended his hand. With cream-colored cloth draped from his shoulders, he resembled a handsome shepherd.

She took hold of his strong arm. "You left me to bathe and you have staked additional skins for shelter."

Gil shook his head. "Not I."

"Mereb then?"

Gil and Naabak both spit out a laugh.

"Your prophet left us these dwellings." Naabak pulled his wife taut to his body. "He has gone to rest and pray."

"Will he return?" Or would he report to her father that she was truly wed?

"I doubt it." Gil led her to the middle tent. One staked between the prophet's and a distant dwelling.

Naabak and Reumah raced each other to the farthest tent. Giggles and shushes followed their shadows.

"Do not worry. Susa will stand guard when we sleep," Gil assured her.

Her face flamed as with fever. "We will sleep?"

Gil leaned down, and his breath teased her ear. "Not for a while, Wife."

29

Gil held open their tent flap and indicated with a gallant sweep of his hand for her to enter first.

Hannah picked at a thread in her gown until it snapped. She wrapped her arms around her waist and rubbed her sides.

"My mother is not here." She trembled as the tent flap closed leaving them alone with a low-burning lamp for light.

"Thank goodness for that." Gil laughed deep and short. The giddy tone to his chuckle had vanished. He moved closer. "You do not need her instruction. Not with me." With steady hands, he removed her gold head band. His eyes held her gaze. He glanced away briefly to keep the prongs from snagging her braids.

Her head covering loosened. The unbound freedom of her temples sent a light shiver down her neck and arms. As the cloth slid from her scalp, her heart slammed against her ribs like a battering ram. "I do not know of such things." Her breaths hurried from her mouth as if she had traveled to the peak of the highest mountain. "What shall I do? To you." Looping a finger under a bracelet, she stroked the gold, pinching it to calm her nerves.

She looked at Gil, and his face did not seem as carefree as when they entered together. "I want to," she assured him. "I've wanted to." She released the bracelet, letting her arms fall to her sides as her confession fell between their bodies.

"Hannah." His face sobered. "I have never."

"Oh." She looked to the mat as he stroked the weave of her hair. "I thought…"

He lifted her chin. "Never. But I have seen livestock in the fields. And when I was old enough, the landowner let me birth the calves. I know enough about mating."

Standing tall, she gave him a smile of assurance. "Since you have the knowledge, I will follow your lead."

The chuckle started low in his belly and bubbled up his chest. "Didn't Reumah tell you anything?"

"She said I would need to remove my bracelets." Gold bracelets clinked as she raised and lowered her arms.

Gil gently grasped her wrist. "I can help you with those." He sat on the mat and his eyes begged her to join him. Sitting on her knees in front of him, she held out her arm. He slipped off the first bracelet. The smoothness of the metal against her flesh sent a tickle across her skin.

"Anything else?" he asked. Another trinket abandoned her skin.

"To remove?"

"That Reumah told you." His warm breath brushed over her fingers. He kissed her hand and held his lips to her skin.

She shook her head. Gil's tenderness drained her of any remembrance. "It happened fast," she blurted out, trying to catch her breath.

"I only work fast in the fields." He flashed a street-thief grin and snatched the last bracelet from her wrist, leaving her arm bare. Holding up a circle of rubies, he said, "This band reminds me of the bracelet you left me as a summons."

She ignored the glint of scarlet in the lamplight. "I left the bracelet for my mother. It was a gift from my father the day I saw the prophet. The day we met." Emotion built behind her eyes. "My mother does not know where I am. Or that we are married. I wish she knew I was safe." A tear slid down her cheek. "And happy."

"Hannah. Wife." Gil's caress on her neck lifted her burden. "You will see your mother when we return home." Gil sought out her tears and erased them with his lips.

How could she tell him of her doubts? What if under religious law she had two husbands? Had her father received a bride price from Azor? Had money changed hands between them? Would lying with Gil be adultery?

She longed to be honest. "If Azor—"

Gil's hand briefly covered her mouth, smothering her words. "We will not speak of him. Not tonight. Tonight, we express our love. The prophet bound you to me and I am going to love you."

Gil tugged off his tunic. He sat bare-chested, in a loincloth.

"Do you want me, Hannah?" He took her hand and drew her splayed fingers down the grooves of his chest. His skin was smooth, with soft, curly hair that felt like wisps of clouds upon her fingertips.

She gripped his shoulder and pressed a kiss to his lips.

"Yes, Gil," she gasped. "I want you." He had stolen a piece of her heart the first day they met when he touched her lip with a pomegranate seed. But at the moment, there was no time for speech.

~*~

When she awoke, Gil was gone. She rested her hand on the mat where his body had lain. The woven reeds trapped his warmth. The previous night had not been a dream. She shivered as she remembered Gil's eager yet tender touch.

A high pitched scrape caught her attention. With morning light piercing through the stitched seams of the tent, she knew someone was at work. Was Gil forced to labor after his wedding night?

The flap of the tent opened. She struggled to sit.

Gil swept into the space beside her, filling it with his presence.

"We will be on the move shortly. Naabak has insisted we honor the Sabbath and rest at sundown." Gil lifted her hand to his lips. "I'm not sure I want rest on this night." The stroke of his palm on the back of her hand sent a stream of energy radiating through her arm.

"Naabak is certainly taking to our ways." She straightened her wayward tunic.

"He will not follow our law to the letter tonight. But with his soldiers camped in the valley below, we must begin our descent."

The scratch of a shovel against rock caused her teeth to ache. "What is going on outside?" She licked her lips. Gil followed the sweep of her tongue with his eyes. She kissed her husband's cheek and smiled as she remembered their time together.

Gil drew her closer. "Mereb is collecting dirt from

the mountain." He pressed his mouth to hers and let his lips linger.

"I did not think Mereb cared for our land." She kissed him softly, yet fully and rose to dress.

Gil leaned back on his arms, his fingers inches from the gold bracelets he had slid from her arms the previous night. "Naabak has ordered that our soil be brought to Aram so he can kneel on it and pray to our God."

"And Konath's body?" Not a twinge of sorrow plucked at her heart.

"Has been wrapped. His family in Damascus would expect it to return."

"I will lead the donkey that carries his remains. The stench will not bother me." She sat and slipped on her sandals. "Is it sinful to be glad he is no longer a threat?"

"I think not since I share your glee." Gil helped her to her feet. "Wife," Gil said with enthusiasm. "We are free. Free to go home to Jerusalem." He brushed her hair from her shoulders. "Let me show you how free we are."

While Gil assaulted her with kisses, the *raatsch* of Mereb's digging barely brushed a nerve. Her heart leapt with delight in returning to Jerusalem, to her home, and to her people. But what would her family say to her coupling with a man from Judah? If her father had promised her to Azor, a Levite, would Shimron announce their union as adultery? Would her brother allow their bodies to be crushed by stone?

She had watched Gil die once while trying to save her life. She would not let him be taken from her again. She would fight for their love. And if they had to die, she would die first.

30

After weeks of hospitality from Benjamin's family, it was time to head south. Hannah would never forget the brave man who saved her from being ravaged in the pit. Benjamin's parents would never forget the couple who had sought his freedom.

Gil and Benjamin brought special offerings to God on the Sabbaths to honor His devotion. Gil shared a portion of Naabak's riches with Benjamin. The comfortable bed Benjamin provided was worth far more than the golden trinkets.

Now, every clop of hooves, every stallion's whinny, brought her closer to Jerusalem. Would there be a feast in honor of her return? A shunning? Or had her brother mourned her death by wild beasts and moved on, awash in temple duties?

The heavy pat on her leg brought her back into the present. The stroke of Gil's hand lessened her hesitation. He touched her often. Often enough that it had become commonplace. But then he had never shied from making her feel whole.

"You are bleeding." Gil pointed to her lip.

She fingered her mouth. Blood bathed her skin. Her anxious spirit had her nipping at her own flesh. She swallowed bits of skin.

"It's of no consequence," she offered as an excuse. Why should she worry Gil about their reception?

They rested the horses in the foothills outside of Jerusalem. Gil picked at a bronze orb embedded in the bridle. Traitorous symbols of Aramean pride accompanied them on their journey home.

"These mounts will bring curious stares." Gil rubbed the bronze medallion. "Our return will reach your father's ears before we stretch our legs."

She surveyed the tiered fields outside the city walls. Squares of brown and green hues blanketed the terrain. She studied a grove of olive trees in the distance, jealous of the shade they cast. "Then let us hide the horses in the grove."

Gil shook his head. "We do not need to sneak into our city." His voice was confident, but the flex of his shoulders told her otherwise.

"Then let us hurry." She urged her horse forward. "So my father is as unprepared as I."

Gil stayed at her side, a few feet in the lead of their pairing. The eastern gate towered over their arrival. Men and women crowded around the city walls. Some called out as if to greet a governor. Who else would ride a bejeweled mount? Hands waved, beating down the rising heat. Hannah pulled on her head covering to shield her eyes so she could concentrate on the narrow street ahead. The road grew smaller and smaller with the girth of the horses and the push of spectators.

A boy, not much older than the one she had seen the prophet heal, ran alongside Gil.

"Can I ride?" the boy yelled, tapping Gil's leg with the familiarity of a brother.

"I have work in the city, Uzzah. Come by later and you can tend to the horses as in the fields."

The boy raced off, no doubt to brag in the alleys.

She caught sight of her aunt, her forehead thick

with a scowl. Feigning a slip in the bridle, Hannah grabbed at the leather strap. Did her aunt blame her own loose lips about the arrangement with Azor for her niece's disappearance? Hannah patted down the mane of her horse and decided it was too late to care.

As they neared her father's two-story house, the temple loomed in the distance. The crowd fell away. Did they fear the chief priest would chastise them for their exuberance? Closer she rode toward acceptance or judgment. Her parents and Shimron waited outside the courtyard wall that surrounded their home. As she viewed her family, the desert air smothered her lungs. Her breaths hitched. Love and longing entwined in her chest.

She and Gil halted their mounts a respectful distance from the dwelling. She slid from her horse and hit the hard ground with a jolt. Gil urged her forward as he tended to the reins. She hurried into her mother's outstretched arms.

"Where have you been?" Her mother's sobs dampened Hannah's tunic. "We thought we had seen the last of you."

She relished her mother's embrace. Her mother began to shift the cloth from Hannah's ear nubs. Hannah stepped back, and left the covering where it lay.

"I traveled north to see the prophet. I waited, but he did not return to us here in Jerusalem." She glanced at her father. Surely he would understand the prophet was her last hope. "I wanted him to heal me and lift the shame I bring to this family."

"You are whole?" her father asked. His worn voice rose with a hint of triumph. He stretched out his arms, ready to join in her mother's embrace.

In all the ways that matter.

"I am not."

Her father's fancy robes buckled at his waist. Her mother wailed. The cry washed over Hannah like a cool rain sending a shiver throughout her body.

"The prophet refused me. He was not harsh." Not at the refusal. She thought it best not to mention the harlot accusation.

"Then it is all the same," her father said. "Azor has agreed to our sum."

"And what of her abundant sins?" Shimron's harsh tone and pointing finger were like the sting of a lash. "Shall she not pay for abandoning her father's household? Deceiving her family? Her mother has mourned. She has brought anguish on the house of Zebula." Her brother's spit wetted her face. He stood on the hem of her skirt. "Azor may not be a forgiving husband."

Gil stepped from the shade of the horses. He seemed to have grown taller in the preceding moments. Bigger. Broader. Bolder. "I am her husband."

"Is this man speaking the truth?" Her father searched her face for validation. Her mother had become a shadow at her father's side.

Shimron clicked his tongue. "You are a laborer. You are not a Levite. What is this wicked scheme?" He whirled on her father. "It is all lies. I saw them together. She did not seek the prophet. She sought out this man. With lust in her heart."

"Gilead is my husband." The affirmation rushed from her lips. Gil stepped closer, showing the reality of their union. His presence renewed her strength. Without his fellowship, her bones would have withered like a shorn leaf.

"How can this be? I did not give my blessing." Her father protested with the intensity of a gale force wind. Anguish wrinkled his face. "This man is not even a kinsman or a priest."

"Hah. He is nothing." Shimron spoke in disregard of Gil's presence. "Who is his father?"

Gil stiffened.

Grasping her father's hands, Hannah beseeched him. "Truly, I sought the prophet. We sought the prophet." She included Gil to show them how much a part of her life he had become. "But we were taken captive in a raid near Mahanaim. By Arameans. Our lives were spared, but I was forced to serve in the commander's household."

Her mother stumbled backward, her face as pale as whitewashed stone. Hannah raced forward and settled her mother on the courtyard wall.

"No harm came to me." Hannah made sure everyone within the city walls was assured of her purity. "The commander of the army gave me to Gilead in marriage. We were not immoral."

"It is against the Law of Moses to be married by a pagan priest." Her brother's voice shook with rage.

Gil pushed Shimron aside. He stood like a strong guard in front of her father. "The prophet of Israel bound us together. On a sacred mountain near Mahanaim. We are husband and wife."

Her father gripped the courtyard wall. "But the prophet knows you belong to the house of Zebula. He knows your heritage as a Levite. I came to him...on your behalf." The grooves on her father's face deepened. Betrayal shrouded his stare.

Should she let the prophet take her father's scorn? No one knew when the man of God would return to

Jerusalem. If ever. Her heart slammed against her ribs as sure and violent as a blacksmith's hammer. She licked her lips, but her palate had become a sheet of linen. *Testify to the truth.*

"It is my doing," she blurted out. Her mother hesitated, but pulled back all the same. "The prophet joined us together because he witnessed something he could not ignore."

"Hannah." Gil's eyes flashed a warning. "What happened on the mountain was a miracle."

"A miracle?" Shimron laughed. "Do confess, Sister."

"Wait." A flicker of understanding brightened her father's gaze. "Can the prophet testify to this miracle? To this act of God?" Her father's question gave her hope.

"Yes." Sweat trickled down Hannah's forehead and cheek. Her vision blurred. Would they believe the craziness on the mountain? "The commander I served was cursed with leprosy. We brought him to see the prophet." She nodded toward Gil. "We had to scale a mountain to seek the man of God. A soldier of Aram struck Gilead with a sword. I called for the prophet and his healing power, but he did not come."

Shimron hissed like a cat.

"I prayed to God." She beheld her father. "The prayers you taught us. When I thought Gilead dead, I mourned him and lay upon his body in grief. I asked God to hear my petition—"

Shimron's hand swept Gil's direction. "You laid on this fool?"

Gil clasped her brother's hand. "It was not in lust."

Shimron grimaced. "Unhand me. Have you no remorse?" Gil let go and Shimron flexed his hand.

"Father, can't you see what they have done? She is no better than a runaway prostitute, except the prophet forced her to be honorable."

"Oh, daughter. What can be done now?" Her mother's countenance crumbled.

"No." Her throat rasped. "Do not say as such. My brother has twisted the truth. I wanted to make you proud. I left to find healing. To have this curse lifted."

"It would seem it is aptly placed." Her father pronounced judgment.

Her eyes filled with tears. "Do you not believe me? I speak in truth."

"Come, Hannah." Gil tugged her gently toward the horses.

Shimron stalked past her to address Gil. "What of the money we promised to Azor to accept a cursed wife? It is not an unhealthy sum. We accepted his livestock. If we do not pay him, he may disgrace your wife in the town square. Or stone her for adultery." The possibility of her death did not seem to bother her brother.

Hannah's chest burned. Could her brother not see past the curse to the sister that played and labored at his feet? His passing glare was as hard as his heart.

She turned to her parents. Certainly they would support her claims in public. All they had to do was talk to the man of God. Had her father given up after years of sacrifices and offerings? "Father? Will you not defend me?"

His expression was firm as baked clay. "We must make good on our debt to Azor. He is a respectable man."

And Gil wasn't? Her father did not speak the words but his demeanor implied them. She could not see her mother's face. Her mother's head covering shielded her grief, but Hannah noticed a renegade tear plunge to the dirt below.

"I will make good on this debt," Gil vowed.

"He speaks the truth." Hannah emphasized her last word. She untied a satchel from her mount and met her brother's skeptical glance. Reaching into the bag, she pulled out the bracelets Reumah had given her. One by one by one she let the gold glimmer in the sun.

Shimron's eyes widened. His hand shot out to claim the wealth.

"Return the animals and any offspring. This should be enough to pay Azor." She intentionally dropped the gem-laden gold bands, one by one by one, into the dirt at Shimron's feet. She flung the last bracelet onto Shimron's dusty sandal.

He flinched as if the metal had branded his flesh and then kicked at her offering.

She slipped Reumah's ruby bracelet onto her mother's wrist. An imposter for her father's gift. The gift that had emboldened her heart. "I'm sorry I disappointed you."

Her mother held onto the bracelet but didn't look up. The silence haunted Hannah's soul.

She unfastened a golden arm band from underneath her sleeve. When it appeared, even her father twitched at the price it would beget.

"If Azor protests, bribe him with this bangle." She held up the gold and let it glisten for a moment before letting it drop with a thud.

Before anyone could question her on where the gold had come from, she mounted her horse. Gil followed her lead. They rode away in haste.

Gil's presence gave her comfort. Together, they would start a new home.

And a new home with Gil was all she needed, wherever it was located.

31

Hannah walked in front of her horse, leaving the bronze-adorned animal to be the spectacle instead of her.

"Mother. Your son has returned," Gil called out as they neared his alley.

Doors opened. Faces peeked from windows.

Just like that fateful day of their meeting, Hannah desired to hide behind the soiled curtain where no one could leer at her.

Jogging to catch up to her husband, she placed a hand on his back and beseeched him to be quiet. "You are calling attention to us."

"As I should. I have returned with a beautiful wife."

His proud grin filled her empty vessel of a body.

The door to her mother-in-law's house flew open. She wondered how long it would take before it would be commonplace to call someone else *mother*.

"Gilead," his mother rasped. Her eyes grew wide and wetted with tears. "You have come home." The attractive woman Hannah had appealed to weeks ago—no, months ago—grabbed hold of Gil's face as if to make sure he wasn't a ghost. "Where did you run off to? I have been burning incense since that first night."

Hannah stood, envying Gil's warm homecoming.

Oh, to have a joyous caress on her face. *I should go to them.* But she did not inch forward. Her body was a scorched reed, chewed on, flattened, and then spit upon the rocks.

"Have you grown?" Gil's mother asked, trailing her hands up and down Gil's arms. She hesitated over a few scars.

"Do not worry. I have been away to see the prophet, but now I am home to stay." Freeing an arm from his mother's hold, Gil extended a hand. "With my wife."

Hannah forced a gracious smile. A smile that hid the sorrow of the last hour.

"My daughter." Gil's mother swung her arms open in greeting. "Come inside." She ushered them off the street and into her home.

Gil hesitated in the doorway. He scanned the small sitting area before entering.

His mother sat on a stool. "There's a chair for your wife in the back room."

Gil headed toward the kitchen like a thief unaware of his surroundings. Her soul ached for him having to live as an outcast with his mother on the other side of a thick wall. He returned with a straight-backed chair. Hannah cherished the seat of honor. Gil sat nearby on some crates.

"I have earned a reward." Gil patted his purse. "Hannah and I helped a wealthy foreigner. Perhaps now I can purchase land from Zadok."

Hannah rested a hand on the expensive weave of her husband's cloak. "He speaks the truth."

Gil's mother leaned in secret-sharing close. The wooden stool she sat on tilted forward. Hannah thought the woman might fall to the floor. "You are the one who came for my son before he left. You are the daughter of Zebula. There was talk in the market that you had gone to Hebron and wedded a priest."

Bright waves of light clouded Hannah's vision. She blinked hoping to regain her sight and clear her head. Did people think she was Azor's wife? "I did not go to Hebron." She wrapped her arms around her waist to keep herself centered on the chair. "Gil and I sought the prophet in Mahanaim. We have been blessed with those coins and each other." She massaged her bare arms. *Oh, God, please let the gold be enough to keep Azor away.*

"The prophet joined us in marriage." Gil's hand massaged her shoulder. His touch made her feel like royalty, not a soiled and cast-off daughter.

Her mother-in-law's hands flew into the air. "*Selah.* We will celebrate tonight. My husband and his sons are away." Excitement shone in her eyes as she straightened her head covering. "I will put leeks in the stew."

"Not on my account." Hannah gave Gil a knowing glance. Her stomach was a tumble of nerves and the flavoring would not tickle her tongue.

"Definitely on your account," Gil said. "We will celebrate as a family."

The pride in his declaration wrapped around her like a golden-threaded scarf.

After dinner and ample apologies from her mother-in-law for being unable to offer lodging, she and Gil headed to his alcove with a blanket for comfort.

"My mother's husband provides a roof for her. It was not provided for me." A hint of sadness was buried deep in his explanation.

"At least your mother did not require a bribe to spare you a stoning. You are a good man, Husband." She hoped her encouragement would lighten his spirits. "You have always been kind to me."

After they dipped under the sheet to his alley, he caught her in an embrace and kissed her so tenderly, the day's worries faded away.

Uzzah's scold of one of the horses rang out on the other side of the soiled-sheet wall.

"Do you need to check on the boy?" Her concern coaxed a handsome smile from her husband.

"He can take care of himself. He has been on his own for a while. Interfering will bring more shouting.

"Is Uzzah an orphan?"

"An orphan in need of work and guidance." Gil smiled as if remembering the boy's prior misdeeds. "I watch over him as does the landowner."

"Zadok seems like a fine man."

"He is, but he prefers if I oversee the boy." He arched his eyebrows. "Zadok has never lived on the streets."

Gil spread the blanket near the rain barrel. "Recline in your palace, my wife."

She sat and leaned against the house wall. Her feet throbbed against the straps of her sandals.

"Now you will have me to watch over. I am an orphan. And this—" She indicated the crates. "Is our bedroom."

"Not for long." He swaddled her with the ends of the blanket.

Tears welled in her eyes. She nestled her face into the crook of his neck.

"Hannah." Her name reverberated from his throat. "Your family is not lost."

His broad chest was a rest to her weary bones. "I knew the consequences when I left. I do not mean to weep. Forgive me. We are together and safe."

His breath was warm upon her ear nub. "Weep for joy my wife, for you have been in my bed too long and not in the women's tent."

Her mind raced.

A chuckle vibrated against her cheek. "It is the truth."

When was her last time? With Reumah. Before they visited the temple of Hadad. She counted the days and weeks. She was overdue. He did not lie.

The alley was dim, even light from the window did not disperse the shadows. But Gil's grin of delight was a beacon in the darkness.

She wished she could fly over the city and sing out her news. "I am carrying your child."

32

Grunts and shouts of stone masons trailed off on the afternoon trade winds. Hannah's new home was almost complete, built on the land Zadok had sold to Gil. She scanned the fields for Uzzah. The boy was taking ample time with his chores.

Two riders caught her attention. Their donkeys were at a full trot. Dirt clouds swirled from the animal's hooves. Had Gil hired more workers?

As the donkeys neared the stable, she realized by the cut of cloth that these men were not laborers. The stiff-backed man in the lead was her brother. The second man with a gray beard long enough to rest on his mount's mane, and an ornate robe coveted by those barred from the most holy of places, could only be Azor.

Warmth flamed across her face. She would have blamed her condition but the babe had never caused her fingers to tremble. Options flashed through her mind. Run inside. Flee to the fields. Hide with the livestock. Thoughts of escape had come too late. Shimron whipped his donkey in her direction.

She glanced over the landscape. No Gil in sight. She held her ground. Receiving two disgruntled priests made her feel like the caged pigeons trapped behind wood as Gil guided their wagon across the Jordan. *God, why do you conspire against me?*

Shimron dismounted. Azor remained seated atop his ride, high and lofty.

"Sister." Shimron's voice was as melodious as a snake charmer's flute. He raised his arms in her direction. Surely, he did not expect an embrace, or worse, a kiss.

She strolled forward and feigned a kiss for formality. "Why is he here?" she whispered through clenched teeth. "Is the gold not enough?"

Shimron pinched her chin, causing her eyes to water. "He would not accept an offering that was likely tribute to a false god."

"Rededicate it if he thinks it plunder." She stepped back, her stomach tightening. She had the pit of a prune burrowing into her belly.

"I made the offer, dear sister." Her brother kept his voice low. "He finds it unacceptable. Apparently in his old age, he values a wife more than coin." Her brother's inflection on the word "wife" made the pounding of the stone masons echo in her cursed ears. "You may sully yourself, but not our lineage. I am the heir of Zebula. My children shall not be disregarded because of your selfishness."

Heat flashed through her body, causing her skin to prickle. She had been honest with her family, not self-serving. "The Blessed One of Israel performed the ceremony on the mountain. I belong to another. Surely he will honor the prophet's proclamation?"

"He questions your truth." Shimron waved Azor forward. "Along with others."

And how would others know of her words? Ignoring Azor's arrogant posture, she took a deep breath. "I have a husband, sir. I have told the truth about our marriage. I do not need two men in my bed."

The *plinking* of the masons halted.

Azor raised a hand as a shield to her anger. "I have the utmost regard for the line of Zebula. Have your father and I not sworn to uphold God's Law? The word of a Levite is trustworthy. However, I have not found a witness to your claims, and I cannot trust a man from the streets. I have no doubt his deception and trickery has swayed your testimony."

Her body quaked with a righteous rage. "How dare you insult my husband. On his land. In front of his workers." She stumbled backward into the arm of a stone mason. He handed her a cup of water. She drank her fill. She did not extend an offer to her guests.

A storm of topsoil clouded the sky. Charging hooves stampeded through the field. The rhythm brought her comfort. Gil had come to her rescue. Again.

Gil jumped from his mount almost atop her brother. He stood in front of her, blocking the sun. His hands-on-hips stance revealed one of Konath's daggers.

"What brings you to the outskirts?" No welcome rang in Gil's greeting.

Azor pulled on the reins of his donkey and lengthened the strap as if readying a whip for an attack. "We have come to discuss your claim to this woman. We can find no witnesses to your union."

"The prophet of Israel gives testimony." Gil's booming voice and the mention of the prophet caused work on the house to come to a standstill.

"No one has seen the prophet since he left Mahanaim for the mountain." Shimron raised an eyebrow inferring she and Gil had something to hide.

She stepped from Gil's shadow. "Did you ask

Makir? The one who leads the army? I spoke with him, face to face, while the soldiers of Aram amassed in the valley. It was Makir who told us where to find the prophet."

"I have kinsmen in Mahanaim." Azor's voice rose with grandeur. "They spoke of our enemies crossing the border. Makir and others gave testimony that they had seen the prophet, and they gave testimony to seeing you, daughter of Zebula. But they could not swear that you had met the prophet."

"We met." Gil stomped toward Azor's donkey like he was meeting a foe in the arena. "If your people have spoken with Makir, then you know we were not alone."

She rushed to Gil's side. "The prophet healed Naabak, the commander of Aram's armies. Naabak's wife, a servant, and a soldier saw the miracle and our marriage." Surely Azor would not persist with such a crowd of witnesses.

"So you have told." Shimron contained his donkey without a care as to the turmoil he had brought to her door.

"Others say a sick man went up the mountain and a dead man came down. How is this the work of the prophet of God?" Azor asked.

"They were not the same man." She threw her hands up in despair. How could she make her brother and the priest believe the truth? She rounded on Shimron. "I am your sister, raised in the same household. Did our parents not instill the Law in us? I will not speak falsely." But she had when it was needed to safeguard her dignity. And Gil's. But they had made atonement. And only God need know of the past. "Do you believe me, your sister, to be a liar?"

"Hah." Her brother's chuckle startled the donkeys. "Do not speak to me of your birthright. You fled in the middle of the night with this man." He flung a wrist Gil's direction insinuating Gil was as bothersome as a tedious fly.

"I sought the prophet to heal my curse." Her secret slipped from her tongue for all to hear. She glanced at the house. Only half the workers seemed to be listening to the argument. "As did our father," she continued, poking Shimron in the chest. Restraint kept her from slapping his face. "Gil saw to my safety."

"He soiled a virgin intended for another," Shimron shouted.

The *tinks* and *tanks* from the masonry work died off completely.

"I am an honorable man." Gil's declaration rang out over the fields. His body shook as it contained his rage.

"Oh, and who will testify to your honor?" Shimron spat at Gil. "Your father?"

Gil's arms rippled. His hand hovered dangerously close to his dagger.

She hugged his waist in a show of love and support as she pointed to the path. "Go. Leave. Now." The force of her command scratched her throat. "Your point is moot. I will not reside with Azor. I am carrying my husband's child."

Shimron's eyes became as wide and dark as a pair of plums.

Azor rode closer, still sitting high on his mount. Hannah put a hand to her forehead to assess his demeanor, but the sun's brightness burned her eyes. Surely he would go now that he learned of the child.

"You are no longer welcome here." Gil jerked free

from her grasp. The jar caused a twinge in her gut. She didn't stop her husband. She couldn't. He muttered insults in Hebrew. Words she tried not to recognize.

"I will not allow God's commandments to be mocked. By law," Azor shouted red-faced, "the child is mine."

"Never." Gil unsheathed his blade.

"Gilead." She called his name like his mother, shrill and strong. No blood would wet this soil. "Husb—" She gagged and bent at the waist. At the force of her call, vomit erupted from her mouth and splattered the donkey's hooves.

Her vision faded. Someone called out her name.

Oh God, do not take my babe.

33

Hannah woke in the bed she and Gil shared as husband and wife. She sat, feeling like a tattered sack emptied of its fruit and thrown on the wood pile. Gil rested in the corner of the room. He had used an old tunic as a mat.

"I did not fare well in the heat. Do they think me demon possessed? Did they flee our land?" Her voice came out deep and rough through her parched throat.

Gil hurried to her side. "They wait. For you." His hand smoothed over her hair and stroked her ear stubs like they were normal. Healed. "How is my wife and our child?"

She placed a hand on her midsection. "I am no longer ill." When she realized her hair was bare of cloth, her heart rallied with hope. "My head covering. Did Azor see my deformity?"

Gil nodded. "But it did not deter his desire to take you from me."

"He has many children of his own. Why does he not return to them?" *Oh, Lord, how much longer will you punish me?*

"Azor will not return home without you." Gil clasped her hands. "And I will not let him take my family."

Tears welled in her eyes. "Can't they leave us alone in our happiness?"

"They will, when we bring witnesses to our union. That is why I am returning to Aram."

Collapsing into his chest, she pulled Gil closer. She slipped a hand into his black curls and wrapped a finger around a lock of thick hair. If only she could anchor him here. Keep him by her side. Root him in the fields. "You cannot leave me. If you do not return…" A tear streamed down her cheek, leaving a trail of wetness and despair before it plunged to the linen below.

"I will return." His voice allowed no doubt. "To you. To my child." His hand slid over her stomach and halted in its middle. "I will not let that haughty Levite raise a rebel from Judah. This child will have my name."

"Your good name." Her throat tightened as she thought of Gil holding their child.

His eyes glistened with pride.

She lightly touched Gil's arm, rubbing the scars of battle. She marveled at her husband's strength. "You have great faith. No one has seen the prophet since we left him. And why would Naabak brave the threat of war to assist a lowly servant?"

He stroked the outline of her face, drying the deserting tears. "I will find them both and they will come. They will beg to return and sing the praises of my wife. What future did Naabak have without you? Without our God? Your prayers even raised a dead man."

She leaned in, forehead to forehead, nose to nose, his breath warming her lips. "Do not give me false hope." She breathed a laugh. "Hope. I thought it had finally come my way. With you." She stretched one of his smooth curls between her fingers and watched it snap back into place. "I have lost all hope. God is still punishing me. But now, in ways more cruel."

"No, you will see." He kissed her wrist. "I will leave tonight for Mahanaim. And if the prophet is not there, I will go to Aram."

"So soon." She did not want to be parted from his warmth.

"It is best." Another kiss bathed her skin.

"Then I will stay and oversee the workers. Our home will be ready—"

"You cannot stay here." Gil's eyes closed as tight as the day she watched him die.

She pulled away. "This is my home."

He sought to draw her back into his arms. "They fear you will ride out to meet me."

"We could do that still."

Gil rested a hand on her shoulder. "Your brother is in the other room and he has threatened to expose us as adulterers if we go against his wishes."

Her stomach churned like a storm-tossed fishing vessel. "I will not share a room or a bed with Azor."

"You will bed with your mother. I have made threats of my own. There are people who will look out for my interests. People who owe me their livelihood."

She bit her lip and withheld her grief. Not one sob rallied from the bed. She wouldn't give her brother the satisfaction of hearing a wail. "How long...how long must I wait?"

"Shimron has given me four Sabbaths."

"Will that be enough?" She clung to his neck, wishing she could drink in the scent of him.

His hands glided from her shoulders to her hips. "If not, look for the boy Uzzah at your window. He will hide you until I return."

She kissed him hard, but with soft lips. Long, but with quick pants. She bunched his tunic in her fists. "I love you."

"And I you," he breathed. "Know that your man of Judah is ready for a fight."

Swallowing the lump in her throat, she whispered, "As is your woman of Judah."

34

The first Sabbath passed.

Had Gil found the prophet in Mahanaim? Had Benjamin agreed to assist Gil? What if Azor's kin had detained her husband and all was lost?

The second Sabbath passed.

Was Gil in Aram? In Naabak's care? Imprisoned or impaled?

The third Sabbath passed.

She prayed that every shout from the street, every bold laugh, every clop of hooves, announced her husband's valiant return. His return with a host of witnesses. Or just one. One who would testify to their union. She was no adulteress.

Two nights before the fourth Sabbath, she was invited to dine on the sacred meats from the day's sacrificial offerings. She sat at a table with her mother and Rebekah. Shimron and Azor lounged nearby. Her father was absent, serving at the temple.

Reumah's bracelets sparkled on Rebekah's arm as she handed Hannah a plate of fatty portions. If the foreign gold was rededicated to God, then apparently God did not have need of it, nor the orphans, nor the widows.

"*Toda*, Sister," Hannah said through thinning lips. "I only want for bread and oil."

"Daughter of Zebula, you are a Levite," Azor

professed. "My clan welcomes you. Eat your fill." His eyes revealed his delight in welcoming her.

Breathe. Out. "I must refuse your kindness, Azor. Although you are gracious, my husband shall return soon."

Shimron chuckled too long. "That thief robbed you of your virginity and rode off to escape punishment. On a stolen horse I might add." Wine spilled from his cup at his final accusation.

A scold teetered on her lips.

Rebekah's daughter wailed.

Hannah remembered her own child and calmed her anger. In a few days, or hours, Gil would return, or Uzzah would come to her rescue. Rest was what she needed if she was to ride into the foothills and sleep on rocks under the moon.

"Forgive me." She rose to her feet. "I am tired." *Tired of your scorn.*

"Sit down," Shimron snapped. "My wife has a child to feed. You can clean the scraps from our table."

She turned to Azor. He acted deaf. He dipped a piece of manna into his stew and chewed it like his tongue needed to taste every nibble.

Gilead. Make haste. "As you wish, Brother."

Later that night, lying in bed, she listened to her mother's restlessness. The rustle of linen on woven reeds reached her ears again and again.

"Daughter," her mother whispered.

Hannah crawled to her mother's side. She held her mother's hand in the dark for comfort. "What is it?'

"I do not want my grandchild living in Hebron." Her mother gave Hannah's hand a snug squeeze.

"Your grandchild will remain in Jerusalem. I am sure of it." She stroked her mother's face.

"I bore no more children after you." Her mother latched onto her arm in a grasp of desperation.

"I know," Hannah said, the guilt of her curse pushing down on her conscience. Had she been so foul to God that her mother's womb was shut? She held her mother close.

After a long while, her mother unraveled from their embrace and searched out a satchel near her mat. Hannah's arm raised and a bracelet slipped over her wrist.

"You left this for me the night you fled, but it belongs to you. Your father would want you to have it. Oh how he tried to make atonement for you."

She kissed her mother's cheek. "I know in my heart he tried."

"He is not here tonight." Her mother cradled her hands with the touch of one holding an alabaster jar of perfumed oil. "I will bless you and your child." A melody, sung in whispered words, rose from her mother's mat. "May the Lord keep you, my daughter. May the Lord make his face shine upon you. May the Lord be gracious to you, and give you peace. Peace, oh my daughter."

And with love bursting forth from her chest, Hannah sang, *"Selah."*

35

Hours later, Hannah awoke with a start. Her heartbeat pounded in her ears like a war drum. Her mother slept oblivious to Hannah's flustered state. As she lay back down, a small rock tumbled from the folds of her tunic. She looked to the window. A silhouette of a face peered over the sill. The form bobbed. An arm motioned in an ecstatic state. Uzzah.

She rose quietly like a seductress slipping out at sunrise. Her mother slept facing the doorway, her back obscuring Hannah's escape. *Forgive me one more time.*

Uzzah helped her jump from the sill. The dark of night was beginning to lift like steam from a summer rain puddle.

"Hurry. My mount is waiting," Uzzah whispered.

She followed Uzzah through the courtyard, to the street. His horse waited two houses away, tied to a bramble bush.

They ran past a house and an alley where she hid from her brother as a child. Dim light glowed from the second house. Shadows shaded the side street.

She jerked to the right. Her arm pinched with pain. She fought to stay on her feet.

"Going somewhere, Sister," Shimron said, loud enough to wake the neighbors.

"Let go." She wrestled against her brother's grip. His fingernails embedded into her flesh with a righteous fury.

"Leave her be." A sling whirled above Uzzah's head. The *whishing* of the leather grew louder.

If only her brother would listen to reason. She did not want to see him hurt, but she would not be the wife of another. She dropped to her knees.

Uzzah released the stone.

Shimron shifted. He shrieked. Blood spurted from his nose.

When her brother's grasp loosened, she pulled free.

Shimron lashed out in a rage. He slammed his fist into her jaw.

She ran. Mouth throbbing, she mounted the horse.

Uzzah aimed another shot.

"Not in the face," she mumbled.

"Now you tell me."

"Harlot," Shimron rasped.

Uzzah readied another assault.

Her brother ducked. "Thief."

Uzzah catapulted onto the mount and slapped its rump. Hannah urged the horse into a run. She didn't look back. She left her brother wounded in the street. She left Azor without a bride. She left without a head covering, free and exposed.

Wind whipped her hair like a flag caught in a breeze. Uzzah buried his face into her back, tickling a spot between her shoulder blades. She smiled. Wetness trickled from her lip. A token from her brother.

They rode at a gallop, past the well, toward the Jaffa Gate.

"Whoa." She pulled back on the reins. Shepherds and sheep, wagons and wagon masters, clogged the square. She weaved the mare in between the masses.

The city gate was closed. A guard stood watch.

"Why isn't the gate open?" she asked a merchant. "I have to get through."

"Only a fool would venture out," the woman answered. "Foreigners are camped in the wilderness."

Gil? Naabak? It had to be. She would find out soon enough. She would not wait for Shimron to sift out the city.

The fortified stone walls of Jerusalem loomed above her.

Uzzah tapped her shoulder. "I know how to escape."

So did she.

36

Hannah rode toward the inn. She planned to walk down the outside of Jerusalem's walls and make it to the foothills before the heat became unbearable. Oh, to rest with Gil. Her true husband. Her true love.

"Hide the horse in the stable in case my brother has begun a search," she said to Uzzah. "You can lower me from the window with a rope."

"In your condition?" Uzzah's voice squeaked.

"I will be fine. I am a woman of Judah now."

"I am afraid of your man of Judah. Harm will befall me if something happens to you."

She motioned for Uzzah to hurry. "I will be safe. I have come this far."

She prayed her man of Judah was camped in the outskirts, for she would not let herself be captured again. If the cupboard was unlocked this morn, she would grab a weapon.

Hannah opened the door to the inn. With dawn's light at her back, there was no need to trick the lock and shoulder it into obedience as Gil had that first night. A few travelers lounged at the table eating morning bread. Hannah's stomach roared at the thought of a meal. An older woman greeted her and offered food. Hannah accepted a small piece of manna. Uzzah snatched a plump raisin cake from the plate.

"We are in need of the window." Hannah nodded

discreetly toward the stairs.

The woman's brow furrowed.

"I have been here before." Hannah didn't want the hostess to think her house was a victim of gossip. "My husband, Gilead—"

"Yes." The woman clasped her hands. She ushered Hannah toward the stairwell before returning to her guests.

Uzzah caught up with Hannah on the second flight. He had a fist crammed with dates.

As she turned to eat the fruit, hushed voices carried down the corridor. Men's voices. Was this a trap? She swallowed and listened. What if Shimron had predicted her route? Did he know of the window? Last time she had fled from this window, she had Gil at her side, not a hungry boy.

Uzzah urged her forward. Had he no fear? Freedom was a few steps away, but what if they faced a fight? *Face it. For Gil. For our child.*

She tiptoed the remaining stairs, trying to retain an element of surprise.

At the top of the stairwell, Uzzah squeezed by her side, his leather strap at the ready. She whipped around the corner, and climbed the small ladder, her young protector close behind.

Talking ceased.

Cloaked heads turned.

She gasped.

"Hannah." Gil, Naabak, and the prophet spoke in unison. Another man with a chest wide enough to wrestle oxen stood next to her husband. It looked like the man had been pulling visitors up the wall for years.

Her muscles went slack. "You're here. In Jerusalem." She blinked several times making sure the men were not an illusion. "Praise God." Emotion strangled her words.

Gil came closer. "How is my wife?" His ardent smile collapsed. His eyes narrowed as he inspected her lip and jaw. "Shimron?" He spit out the name like a curse.

"He tried to keep me from leaving. Though, his face looks far worse than mine. Uzzah is precise with a stone." She rocked on the heels of her sandals, longing to be scooped into Gil's arms, his strong, loving arms.

Leaning in, Gil whispered, "Later, I will show you how much you have been missed." The rumble in his voice caused warmth to sweep from her neck into her cheeks.

Uzzah stomped his foot. "What of my bravery? Her brother crouched in the alley, ready for her flight."

Gil rested a hand on Uzzah's head. "I would have been here days ago if I traveled alone." Gil nodded slightly toward the prophet. "But I knew you could slip in and rescue my wife from a house of priests."

Naabak laughed. "Do we not venture to see the same priests?"

She turned and marveled at her former master. His skin was the color of walnut shells not seeping sores. His beard had grown thick and black from his chin to his defined nose. She bowed out of habit mostly, but also gratefulness. "You came all this way. For me. Am I truly worth all this trouble?"

Naabak raised his arms. His cloak fell away exposing an ornate breastplate. "Oh, Israel, Look at me. I am alive. Strong. Truly in command of all the armies of Aram. My wife is expecting an heir, as are you I am told."

Had she heard Naabak correctly? She would bear

a son? An overly content grin radiated from Gil's face. Naabak must be truth telling. Did the prophet reveal this knowledge during their travels?

"I would be buried in a tomb if you did not tell me of your God," Naabak added.

"I am blessed that you have come. Truly we have need of your testimony. But I do not want to be the cause of a war between our people."

The prophet sighed. "Neither Israel, nor Judah, will attack with the Sabbath so near. If they do, they will sense the Lord is not with them. If I speak on behalf of Aram, what leader would dare risk their men? I persuaded the commander to come to the temple."

She grasped Naabak's solid hands. Gone was the mutilated flesh of leprosy. "May our God bless you for the kindness you have shown to me and my husband."

Naabak squeezed her hands. "It is much easier to show kindness to you." He pursed his lips. The gratitude in his eyes shone brighter than any gems she had brought back from Damascus.

"I carried you up the mountain." Gil clapped a hand on the commander's shoulder.

"And you enjoyed drowning me in the cistern." Naabak looked to the prophet resting on the window sill for allegiance.

Gil released Naabak's arm and flailed his hand in jest.

"But I didn't let go." Gil's carefree laughter filled the room.

Hannah relished the teasing. She stepped back into a pile of ropes and caught her balance. Her relationship with Naabak had changed since the mountain. Fear did not seize her, nor did despair. Friendship had found a way into her heart, and it would seem after this journey, that friendship had found its way into Naabak's heart as well.

Gil stepped to her side. "I agree with my wife's blessing. You have traveled from your home and we are in your debt."

"Ah, but my task is not finished." Naabak glanced out the window toward the foothills.

The prophet rose from the sill. "If we are to go to the temple, we will need drapes for your swords. I do not want a riot."

"I will see to it." The burly man headed for the stairs.

"How about a rag for Judah's mouth," Naabak called after the innkeeper.

The prophet pointed his staff at Uzzah and directed him to assist the host.

Hannah smoothed a hand over her hair. She did not want to face her brother bare-headed. "I will need a covering as well." Her joy tempered. She still wore the brand of adulteress.

Shimron, her brother, her accuser, and her judge had been wounded by the sling of her rescuer. She had to get to the temple before Shimron rallied a crowd to stone her. She would not watch Gil die trying to save her. Not again. Never again.

The prophet prodded her shoulder with his staff. "The house of Zebula must be set straight. Are you fearful, Daughter?"

She shook her head. "The God of Israel has spared me from worse than this. How can I be afraid with two warriors at my side and God's messenger to speak on my behalf?

The prophet stiffened. "Who said I would be

doing   the   speaking?"

37

She trailed Gil and Naabak as they made their way through the marketplace. The prophet plodded on ahead. His staff kept pace with his steps. Staff-foot, staff-foot, staff-foot.

The square buzzed with more bickering than bartering. Few tambourines rattled to gain a buyer's attention. The beat of the timbrel thudded like a death march. Soldiers camped in the hills, worried merchant, tradesman, priest, and parent alike.

A line of people waited in the outer courts of the temple. Heads turned her direction. Whispers began. Worshippers stepped backward, either because of her lineage or because of the generous swing of the prophet's staff. If they only knew who her cloaked companions were, they would have fallen prostrate.

"Where is her offering?" a man asked.

Her father had brought her to the temple day after day, month after month, year after year. She hiccupped with sorrow as she remembered how her father held fast to the belief that one day she would be made whole. She longed to scream, "Look. At my ears. My mouth. My nose. I can smell your ram, your incense, your roasted grain. The house of Zebula is downcast no more." For now, it was for naught.

"Hannah."

She found the prophet staring at her. Had he

heard her thoughts of vindication?

"Let us go up to the altar. Your father awaits."

Hannah cast a glance at the stairs leading to the upper courtyard. The stone steps loomed like the jaws of a lion waiting to devour the cursed who dared approach the sacred sanctuary where God tabernacled with His priests. Testing every step, thinking it might disintegrate under her sandal, she ascended through the smoke from burnt offerings. Fire flashed from the altar perched above the flight of stairs. The clouded air caused her to cough. Gil braced one of her arms. Naabak braced the other.

"Zebula," the prophet shouted from the top of the stairs. Her family name echoed to the top of the bronzed columns of the temple building.

The priest in the linen ephod turned around. His three-pronged altar fork clattered to the ground.

"Azor," she gasped. Her heart sped. Heat flooded her body. She clamped onto Gil's arm.

"You seem surprised, daughter of Zebula." Azor spoke in a loud, chastising voice. "Is your father not grieved? Your brother not unclean due to the blood you drew from him? Have these men brought you to honor your father's vow?"

Worshippers gathered near their priest and bombarded Hannah with the hiss of their insults.

She had carried the threat of a union with Azor to Aram and back. A public outcry would not sway her decision. Her patience with her elderly suitor strained.

"I am bound to this man of Judah."

Gil pulled off his hood and gave the crowd a stern-faced warning.

"I have brought witnesses to our union," she said. "I spoke this truth to my family, but it was treated as foolishness." Her throat burned as she defended her marriage. *Oh, if I could have the prophet's staff to hold me upright.*

The prophet whipped off his head covering and flung it on the altar. A whoosh of flame engulfed the grate.

People screamed. Some scattered. Others prayed.

"Blessed One." Azor fell to his knees and bowed in reverence. "I did not see..." His apology evaporated into his ephod.

"Seize her." The command echoed through the upper courtyard.

Hannah shook at the harshness of her brother's order. Did he not care that the prophet was in her midst? She glanced at the stairs. They tempted her to flee. Fire raged from the altar, but she held fast to her husband. She held fast to Naabak. She held fast to the truth.

Shimron ushered two temple guards forward. His bow to the prophet was as brief as a horse's head buck.

Gil widened his stance. She could not see his hand but there was no doubt in her mind that it rested on his dagger.

Naabak's drape flew to the side and settled to the ground like a dying moth. He unsheathed his sword.

The crowd gasped, but they were too astonished to flee.

Naabak threatened Shimron and the guards with the blade. "I owe a debt to this woman. I left land and love to speak on her behalf." His polished breastplate shimmered in the sun as he stalked closer to her brother. "Don't you want to hear what I have to say?"

"I do." Her father shuffled from the court of the holy places and bowed low to the prophet.

Hannah bit her lip to keep from sobbing. She kept silent and let Naabak have his say.

"I was a corpse when this woman first beheld me." Naabak displayed his build and armor for all the onlookers to see. "Disease ate at my limbs. This woman did not shy away from my ugliness. She touched me with herbs. Remedies from God. She did not fear my disease. She told me of your prophet and his powers. I stand here today because what she said was true. Your prophet healed my leprosy. The strength of your God saved me." Naabak paced in front of her father and brother daring them to challenge his word. "I gave this woman to this man as the prophet willed. They wed under the eyes of our God."

The prophet stood in front of her father, steadying himself with his staff. "It seems I caused confusion binding your daughter to the Judahite on the mountain and allowing this foreigner"—the prophet jabbed his staff at Naabak—"to take your place."

"Then it is true. My daughter cannot eat at the table of the Levites." The hem of her father's ephod pooled in the dirt. The disappointment in his eyes saddened her soul.

"I cannot eat the fatty portions." She stepped away from Gil and joined the prophet. "But my husband is a good man. One who honors God. I have seen God work miracles through him. The Most High God answered my prayers, and spared Gilead's life, and the commander's life. He even spared my own life. Is life not more precious than the choice fat from burnt animals?"

The prophet stamped his rod. "Hear O Israel."

Her father's wrinkled face filled with tears. "I should have pursued the prophet that day. I tried, my daughter. I truly did. It seems I gave up too soon."

Naabak lowered his sword. "If you had pursued the prophet," he said to her father, "I would have died. My line cut off. Your daughter brought me new life. She gave hope to Aram."

"She gave comfort to an enemy of Israel." Shimron's outrage returned once Naabak's splendid sword was sheathed. "This pagan is nothing more than a spy."

"He saved my life and the life of my husband." Her rebuke rose high as if on seraph wings.

Naabak gripped her brother's arm. He jerked Shimron into an embrace, nose to breastplate. "Greetings to the House of Zebula."

"Aagh." Her brother drew back and covered his nose.

The temple guards retreated.

"You are bleeding, Shimron." Her father did not face his son. "Remove yourself from the temple at once and wash your scrape. Furthermore, you are unclean."

"And, brother," Gil called out, "those bracelets you kept were a gift from the commander's wife. See that *my* wife receives them in haste."

"In haste," Naabak echoed. "That is an order from a brother in Aram."

"It is not too late, Zebula." The prophet urged the chief priest forward. "You can still seek the healing of your daughter. Is it not your duty to call on God for our people?"

Her father reached out and stroked a lock of her loose hair. His hand trembled as if he had caught a chill. His gentle touch caused her throat to constrict. Her legs became like satchels of grain, heavy and awkward. She closed her eyes, unable to behold the

241

anticipation in her father's gaze.

Her father kissed her forehead. Not a quick kiss. His kiss lingered like all the years of anguish. "Receive God's blessing, daughter of mine." His breath wisped upon her skin. "Be healed in His sight, and mine."

The darkness behind her eyelids flashed with light as luminous as a freshly oiled lamp. No pain sizzled on her skin, only a spring-day warmth that touched her flesh, but caused no burn. Her head covering lifted from her hair. She stilled.

When she opened her eyes, her father's hands shot skyward. He sobbed the *Shema*. The crowd joined in to cover his crying.

"I am clean?" Tears welled in her eyes and spilled freely as if they too were released from a burden. She licked her lips and her tongue tingled, front to back, side to side. Threading her fingers into her hair, her touch rose up hills, over cliffs, and dipped into valleys as she caressed her ears. She giggled at the strange sensation of being the same as everyone else. "I am whole."

Gil stroked her ears. "I believe you will be needing jewels for those lobes. I will set a fair price."

She giggled through tears as he imitated the daring merchant that had sought her in the street.

"But hear me, Wife." His voice lowered to a rumble. "I always thought you beautiful. From your dark eyes and stern nose, to your lips the color of celebratory wine. When we met, you were brave and did not run from me. You cared about my hunger."

Hugging Gil's neck, she breathed him in for the first time. The scent of his skin bolstered her boldness and spiked a tingle to her toes. "I am glad I did not run from you." Before she released her husband, she whispered, "We will be together tonight."

The prophet raised his staff. The people quieted. "Behold the daughter of Zebula. Our God has answered her prayer." The prophet turned to her father. "And your prayer, Zebula."

Turning from Gil, she embraced her father. She embraced him as tight as the first day he brought her into the temple. "You healed me."

"The Lord healed you. Not I." Her father's chest vibrated as he wept. "Why he did not do it sooner, I do not understand."

"I may speak for God, but even I do not know His mind," the prophet said. "If I was allowed to heal her on the first day, would she have dwelled in Aram? Called out to God, not for herself, but for others? She would not have left Jerusalem." The prophet poked Gil in the chest with his staff. "Woe that she left it with him."

Naabak laughed so loud he sounded like a stubborn donkey.

Gil winked at her and elbowed Naabak.

Azor strolled forward from the altar and touched the sleeve of her father's robe. "I went to my kinsman because your son cast doubt on the testimony of my intended. I have no doubts now. She belongs to another."

"I did not mean to cause you hardship." Hannah looked to Azor, and then to her father. "The house of Zebula will make it right with you."

Her father nodded.

Azor bowed to her family before returning to his duties.

Gil stepped to her side and cleared his throat. She had never seen Gil so serious. Not even when he spoke about his mother.

"Our first introduction did not go so well, Father. I assure you I will take care of your daughter and the children God grants us. We have land and a modest home not far from the city."

Her father's head bobbed as he dried his eyes. "You may not be a Levite, but you are a fine Hebrew. You brought my daughter home."

"Speaking of home," Naabak interrupted. "My men are waiting."

The prophet picked up Naabak's cloak. "Come and follow me." He prodded Hannah in the back and then turned his staff on Gil. "We have time for a meal in the upper room before you lower Naabak and me to the ground."

"You are leaving Jerusalem?" The question flew off her tongue.

"Our God is not limited by borders. I have work to do in Aram." The prophet turned toward her father. "Trust that I will return."

"Join us, Father." She held out her hand. "Send a servant for Mother."

Her father hesitated and looked to the doors of the temple. "Yes. We will sing praises. We have much to be thankful for. The house of Zebula is cursed no more."

She had never seen her father move so fast nor had she been embraced so tight. But it was his laugh. A laugh she could not remember hearing. A laugh she would never forget. For her father's laugh was as big and bold and just as beautiful as the laugh from her man   of   Judah.

Epilogue

Ten months later

Hannah rested her weight on her elbows and tried to listen over the gurgle of the stream. "Did you hear a cry?"

"There is no one near." Gil rolled on his side, wrinkling the blanket, and kissed the top of her hand. "If we return to the house, your mother will scold. She learned of my mother's stay with the baby. Joel has been fed and will sleep while we rest."

She gazed at the lush fig trees and breathed in their roasted grain and sweet citrus scent. They were as full and green as Gil had relayed on the mountain. "How different this place is than the dark caves."

"I do not care to remember our journey to Aram." A well-placed kiss on her neck brought her focus back to her husband. "I only care to remember your promise to come here with me."

"When Naabak barely lived, I did not think I would see this place on this side of heaven." She smoothed the cropped hair of his beard. "Will we ever see him again?"

Gil's face turned thoughtful. "I have no desire to leave my family or my land."

"Nor do I." She reached into her satchel and offered a pomegranate to Gil. "If you're hungry, this fruit is sweet."

Gil raised an eyebrow. "How do you know? Did you glean it?"

"No. I tasted a tiny piece."

"It won't pucker my lips?" He flashed a do-you-remember grin.

"It won't." She stroked his cheek. "But I will."

Here's a sneak peek at Barbara M. Britton's
upcoming release. . .

Building Benjamin: Naomi's Journey
Coming Feb 2017

1

In those days Israel had no king; everyone did as they saw fit. ~ Judges 21:25.

Shiloh, in the land of the tribe of Ephraim

Naomi peeked from behind the tent flap. Girls emerged from scattered booths, illuminated by the flames of the bonfire. The beat of a timbrel echoed over the vineyards while tambourines tinked in thanksgiving to God for an abundant crop. Naomi's stomach hollowed at the thought of joining in the revelry at the harvest celebration. She had never danced before at the feast in a manner to seduce a husband.

Her palms dampened. It was almost time. Time to twirl and catch the eye of a landowner. With two of her brothers slain by the Benjamites, her father needed a bride price.

Movement in the moon-shadowed vineyard caught Naomi's attention. Had a goat gotten loose among the vines? She squinted into the darkened rows of naked stalks. No leaves shook. No trellis gave way. No bleating rang out. *The smoke is deceiving me.* She blinked and retreated from the open flap.

Cuzbi, the merchant's daughter, came close as if to share a secret. Naomi's reflection widened in the gold of Cuzbi's headband. "Do not worry," Cuzbi whispered. "Follow me and the men will line up to give our fathers gifts."

Naomi prayed this was not a lie. Cuzbi had danced the previous harvest, and the one before, but Cuzbi's father had not received a single shekel.

Naomi smoothed a crease in Cuzbi's striped robe. "I will dance in thankfulness to God for a bountiful harvest and let my brother and father deal with any suitor. You will be the bride tonight. I hope your father is prepared for an onslaught."

Cuzbi squared her shoulders, growing even taller. She patted her hip. Jeweled rings glimmered on every finger. "Come, Naomi. Stand as if a jar rests on each shoulder. The drape will show your curves."

Naomi's nerves fluttered like a wounded dove. She brushed a hand over her ringlets. A lone braid kept her curls from obscuring her face. Losing her brothers' wages meant more time at the loom and less time adorning her hair. Her dyed sash would have to entice the spectators, for unlike Cuzbi's adorned robe, Naomi's was pale as a wheat kernel.

Before she could check her appearance in her polished bronze mirror, Cuzbi grabbed Naomi's arm and jerked her out of the tent.

"The men will arrive soon from their feasting." Cuzbi's gaze darted about the clearing as she surveyed the ring of virgins who pranced around the fire. Young women in colorful linen swayed to the music. "Ah, there is an opening near the front of the procession." Cuzbi sprinted into the circle.

Naomi raced after her friend and ducked nearer the fire, next to Cuzbi. Dancers bumped Naomi's side, jostling to be seen by their mothers and ultimately the eligible men making their way from the banquet.

Hurry, Father. How much roasted lamb and wine did the men of Ephraim need?

Waving to her mother, Naomi signaled her arrival into the mass of whirling bodies. A bead of sweat trickled from her temple and slithered down her cheek. She swiped it away and raised her hand in praise to God. She lifted the other and pretended to card wool in the wind.

Cuzbi leapt in the air and swung her arms as if they were waves rolling off the Jordan River.

Not ready to leave the hard ground, Naomi kicked up her heels one at a time, careful not to injure any followers. Her stomach balked at any elaborate jumps.

A scream rose above the music. Then another.

Had someone fallen? Been burned by the fire?

From the fields, half-naked men wrapped in loincloths rushed into the circle of dancers. Naomi froze, even though the tempo of the timbrel remained festive. These were not the bathed and robed men of Ephraim coming to celebrate. These were armed warriors. She breathed a prayer of praise that her surviving brother imbibed at the banquet.

A charging intruder whipped a sling her direction. Covering her head, she crouched under the *whoop, whoop, whoop* of his weapon.

"God protect me," she prayed.

Music stopped. Wailing started. Naomi looked up. A raider scooped Cuzbi off her feet. He slung her over his shoulder as if she were a small child.

"*Regah.* Stop!" Naomi screamed.

The strong-armed man vanished into the surrounding vineyard with her friend.

Another assailant plucked a virgin from the scramble of dancers. Naomi reached to grab hold of the girl's outstretched hand, but a bear of a man blocked her rescue. His weapon whirred in flight above his head. Naomi dove to the side and crashed to the ground, careful to avoid the flames.

Crawling like an asp over a flat-topped boulder, she headed for the fields. A raider grasped at her sleeve. His nails scraped her skin. Pain sizzled down her arm as if embers from the fire had embedded in her flesh.

"*Kelev. Kelev katan.*" The high-pitched insult grew closer. Naomi glanced backward. A scowl-faced boy ran toward her attacker.

Her young savior slashed a pointed stick at the assailant, snaring the leather sling. She had seconds to escape. Praise be to God!

She fled into the harvested rows of vines—in the opposite direction from where Cuzbi had been taken.

Racing along the rows of plants she'd played among as a child, Naomi's heart lodged in her throat, strangling each breath.

Curses trailed after her. Curses about her speed. Curses in…Hebrew? Her own tongue?

Banking right, she panted as if these bandits had also stolen the night air. She sprinted toward the broken trellis, needing a shortcut through the barricade of vines. If she made it to the olive grove, hiding would be easy among the trunks and branches. Had her sole remaining brother been lazy? Or had he replaced the worn trellis before his revelry? She prayed he'd forgotten his duties this once.

Her hand hit the cracked wooden rod. Splintering, it gave way. "*Selah*," she exclaimed under her breath, for this one time, her brother's laziness was praiseworthy.

Ducking under the greenery of the grape plants, she darted toward the station of olive trees. Her sandals *thapped* against her heels. Certainly the raider would hear her flight, but slowing her pace would put her in peril. Oh, where were the men of Shiloh? Her father? Her brother? And why were these warriors invading a religious celebration?

She passed one olive tree. A second. A third. A fourth. With trembling hands, she beat at the shoots from a tree and buried herself amidst the leaves. She listened for her follower. No footfalls. Good. Her chest burned, greedy for air.

Leaves rustled.

She stilled, but couldn't silence her breaths. In and out they rushed, sounding like a saw on cedar. Old-growth trees were not far away. She scrambled down another aisle for better cover. Grabbing an olive branch, she propelled herself behind a trunk. She hit something hard. The bark? Her forehead ached as though a rock had pelted her skull. Flickers of flame dotted her vision.

When she went to massage her temple, someone seized her arm.

Her stomach cramped. "Leav—"

A palm smothered her lips. The taste of salt and soil seeped into her mouth. Her back struck the prickly growths from the tree. Protests lodged in her throat. Darkness surrounded her, but she kicked at where her captor's legs should be. Banishing the dainty kicks of the dance, she thrashed to do damage. Her attacker did not turn aside. He pinned her to the trunk and held fast.

Lewd taunts grew closer. Her pursuer from the vineyard was in the grove.

Oh, God, do not let me be defiled by one man, let alone two.

"Answer me quietly. Are you one of the virgins?" Her captor's command came forth in Hebrew. He lifted his hand from her mouth, leaving barely enough space to answer.

"Let me go." Her breath rushed out as if it too were fleeing these raiders. "I will slip away. I promise not to alert my people."

"Shhh." Her captor pressed his warm palm over her lips.

"Virgin. Step forth."

Instantly, she was pulled to the ground. Her captor pinned her hips to the dirt with his weight. He lifted her robe. Cool air bathed her knees, sending a chill throughout her body.

She fisted his hair. "Spare me." Even with all her strength, she could not remove him from her body. Her heart pounded louder than a ceremonial drum.

He caged her in the dirt and sent his lips crashing into hers.

She squirmed. Her stomach lurched. Her lungs ached. She needed a breath. She needed a savior.

His weight pressed against her belly. Though he did not take her hem above her thigh. And he did not take her virginity.

"*Argh.*" A roar split the night sky. "Eliab, what are you doing?" The bear-man stood over them, huffing from his pursuit.

Her captor finished his kiss. "Lie still." His words rumbled against her ear. The side of her face prickled from his stubble.

"You mean what *have* I done?" Her captor's body continued to cover hers. "I have taken a wife."

He had not! This man, Eliab, had rested upon her, but he had not joined with her. Although if her father or brother caught him atop her, they would beat him until he claimed her as a wife, or offered a hefty sum. She was not about to call Eliab a liar with her pursuer from the fire crouched over them, staring wickedly. Why had Eliab lied? Was he a friend to the tribe of Ephraim? A friend to a tribe of Israel?

"Go on, Gera." Eliab rose, bearing his weight on his forearms. "Find another. We must leave at once. Hurry. Or do you care to look upon another man?" Eliab's question shot out like a well-aimed arrow.

Gera hesitated. He spat at Eliab's feet and retreated toward the bonfire.

Her spine sank into the ground. Thanks be to God. She reached to right her robe.

Eliab gripped her wrist tighter than a gold band. Realization of his intent sent her heartbeat on another gallop. He had not been a brute, yet he held her prisoner, and he did not seem set on releasing her.

"I am in debt to you. And you will be in debt to my father if he finds you touching me." She tugged against his rigid arm. Her cheeks warmed like stones near a fire pit. "Let go."

"I cannot deny a fellow Benjamite a wife and then fail to claim her for myself." With a jerk, he coiled her into his chest.

Naomi stiffened. The thud, thud, thud in her ears grew louder. "You are a murdering Benjamite?"

"One of the few that remain after the slaughter." His words were sharp as a blade.

Naomi picked up her feet in hopes Eliab would be pulled off balance. He remained rooted to the soil.

"Have you come for revenge?" She grunted her

question while struggling to free herself. She squinted into the vineyards. No legion of rescuers ascended the raised beds. Did the men of Shiloh believe this raid a hoax? "There cannot be enough Benjamites left alive to stand against one tribe of Israel, let alone all the tribes."

"I risked a raid for my survival. Benjamin will not be cut off from God. Our women and children have been slain. Our men ambushed in battle. Are we to have no heirs?" The anger simmering in his reply caused a shiver to rattle her bones.

She thrashed like an unruly child. Eliab held firm. "You were kind to spare me from your Gera. Now double that kindness and let me be on my way."

"Gera's kinsmen brought destruction on our tribe. If a name is to suffer extinction, it should be his, not mine." Eliab yanked her off her feet and heaved her over his shoulder. Her temples pulsed as blood rushed to her brain. Fainting would only make his escape easier. She closed her eyes and concentrated on the darkness.

He cinched his hands around her calves and ran. Fast. His shoulder bludgeoned her belly with every jump and jolt. Her stomach spewed up manna and grapes, burning her throat, and muffling her screams.

When his collarbone was about to impale her side, he righted her next to a mule hidden from sight among the brush. She slumped to the ground.

"If you steal me away from my father, God will punish your sin." Vomit welled in her throat. She swallowed hard. "I did not finish the harvest dance."

Eliab crouched in front of her. His eyes were dark as a clouded night sky and held no mercy. "If I do not take you, one of Israel's tribes will cease to exist. God has more to be angry about than a missed seduction."

Tears blurred her vision. She swung a fist at him, but he dodged her attack. She clawed at his tunic. At least she did not have to fear loosening a loincloth like those scantily clad attackers near the bonfire. "How dare you rip me from my home? Benjamites killed two of my brothers. Do not take the daughter of a grieving man."

He pried her fingers from his garment and pulled her close. "And what will your father do if he believes you are no longer a virgin?"

"There was no union." She beat his chest for emphasis. Her knuckles bruised, yet he barely moved.

He pressed his thumbs into her palms and stilled her assault. "No one will bless a union with a Benjamite. No one will give us their daughters. We are left to kidnap Hebrew women. Since I stole you, your father will be held blameless before the elders of the tribes." He stood and yanked her to her feet.

"My father needs a bride price to buy land." Her words rushed forth. She grabbed his arm. "You have lost family and so have I. Have we not both suffered? Leave me here and be on your way."

"Others may not have been rewarded with a mate tonight. Shall I send you into their bed and disappoint my father?" No joy rang from his words. He did not seem giddy like a bridegroom in a marriage tent.

She stepped backward. Could she outrun him in the darkness? She had to. This was her home. Her land. Her tribe.

He caught her wrist and wrapped it with rope. Stray strands scratched her skin.

"Please." She tensed her muscles and pulled against his weight to no avail. Tears wet her cheeks as he bound her other wrist. "My family—"

"Most of my family is buried in a mountain." He unhitched the mule and snapped the reins.

Her body stilled as if encased in clay. Eliab wasn't listening to her hardship.

Distant shouts echoed from the vineyard.

"Father." Her voice squawked like a strangled pigeon.

Eliab stifled her shouts with a rag. "You can ride the mule or I will drag you behind it. Decide. Now." He turned toward the road. "Hoist the nets."

Was he going to trap her kin like wild beasts?

In a blur, he mounted his ride, still holding the rope as if she were a wayward goat.

How could she leave Shiloh? Leave her mother? Leave her father? Her legs trembled as if the ground shook. She did not take a step.

The mule trotted forward.

With no arms for balance, she fell on her side. Her jaw ached from the gag. Coughing, she tugged on the rope and struggled to rise. If he kicked the animal, she would be dragged through rock and dirt.

Eliab dismounted, swept her into his arms, and sat her sideways on the mule. He had caught her and now he caged her with reins at her back and reins at her chest. His body imprisoned her. He leaned into her arm and slapped the mule's rump. "Hah."

She grabbed the animal's mane, weaving her fingers into the coarse hair for balance.

How could the tribe of Benjamin thieve wives from the tribe of Ephraim? Where was their honor? Where was their shame? And where was God? The feast this night was in His honor.

While Eliab was intent on the terrain, she worked a silver band from her finger and let it slip down her leg, down the mule's withers, to the ground. She would leave a trail for the men of Shiloh.

For what was lost could be found.

Thank you...

for purchasing this Harbourlight title. For other inspirational stories, please visit our on-line bookstore at www.pelicanbookgroup.com.

For questions or more information, contact us at customer@pelicanbookgroup.com.

Harbourlight Books
The Beacon in Christian Fiction™
an imprint of Pelican Ventures Book Group
www.pelicanbookgroup.com

Connect with Us
www.facebook.com/Pelicanbookgroup
www.twitter.com/pelicanbookgrp

To receive news and specials, subscribe to our bulletin
http://pelink.us/bulletin

May God's glory shine through
this inspirational work of fiction.

AMDG

You Can Help!

At Pelican Book Group it is our mission to entertain readers with fiction that uplifts the Gospel. It is our privilege to spend time with you awhile as you read our stories.

We believe you can help us to bring Christ into the lives of people across the globe. And you don't have to open your wallet or even leave your house!

Here are 3 simple things you can do to help us bring illuminating fiction™ to people everywhere.

1) If you enjoyed this book, write a positive review. Post it at online retailers and websites where readers gather. And share your review with us at reviews@pelicanbookgroup.com (this does give us permission to reprint your review in whole or in part.)

2) If you enjoyed this book, recommend it to a friend in person, at a book club or on social media.

3) If you have suggestions on how we can improve or expand our selection, let us know. We value your opinion. Use the contact form on our web site or e-mail us at customer@pelicanbookgroup.com

God Can Help!

Are you in need? The Almighty can do great things for you. Holy is His Name! He has mercy in every generation. He can lift up the lowly and accomplish all things. Reach out today.

Do not fear: I am with you; do not be anxious: I am your God. I will strengthen you, I will help you, I will uphold you with my victorious right hand.

~Isaiah 41:10 (NAB)

We pray daily, and we especially pray for everyone connected to Pelican Book Group—that includes you! If you have a specific need, we welcome the opportunity to pray for you. Share your needs or praise reports at http://pelink.us/pray4us

Free Book Offer

We're looking for booklovers like you to partner with us! Join our team of influencers today and receive at least one free eBook per month. Maybe more!

For more information
Visit http://pelicanbookgroup.com/booklovers

She ignored his insult and watched his blade, anticipating any move in her direction.

He skillfully sheathed the knife with one hand and shoved it back into his sack.

"Go on, take it." He inched the fruit closer to her mouth.

"I have nothing to trade." Hannah crossed her arms and burrowed them against her waist. "And I do not want for food."

He bit off a chunk of pomegranate and swallowed. "The cost doesn't matter. I gleaned it."

"Then I shouldn't take it from you if you are allowed to glean with the poor," Hannah said. *This may be the only food he has all day.*

He shook his unruly hair and dropped his satchel near her. "I am not poor. I offer protection during the harvest. And I can tell by the weave of your tunic and your ruby bracelet, you are not in want."

Hannah glanced at her wrist. Scarlet gems sparkled at the edge of her sleeve. The bracelet hadn't stayed hidden. Why couldn't anything go right today?

In an instant, he reached out and brushed the pomegranate against her lips.

Flinching, she bumped her shoulder bone against the wall.

"You touched it. Now eat." He tilted his head and grinned as if he dared her to challenge his hospitality.

She hesitated, rubbed her arm, and accepted the fruit.

Slumping next to his bag, he leaned into the wall and kicked out his legs. His fingertips pursued the pomegranate's berries.

Hannah eased down the wall and sat near him. The man's closeness caused a tingling along her side

"There you are. Have we not suffered enough today?" Her brother clamped down on her wrist and noticed the piece of pomegranate in her hand. "Where did you get that?"

A shiver shook her arm. "From—"

"Me," Gil said, stepping forward. His arched back broadened his shoulders.

Her brother's glare raked over Gil. "He is filthy. Has he kept the ceremonial laws?" Her brother shook the fruit from her hand. Dirt coated the saliva-soaked peel.

Gil bent to pick up her piece of pomegranate. He drew to her brother's height and bested it. "You cannot judge me."

Hannah cut off her brother's reply. "Gilead showed me hospitality. We owe him better."

"Not much," her brother jeered.

Pain pulsed down her arm from her brother's grasp. He hurried her up the street. When she looked back, Gil had started after her. There was no more moonlight in his eyes.

She whipped around, broke free from Shimron, and ran toward Gil. Her family did not need another scene in the streets. "Do not pursue us," she whispered. And louder, "*Shalom.*"

Gil glanced at her brother and then handed her the dropped fruit.

Shimron flanked her side. "She is not worth your concern."

Hannah met Gil's questioning gaze. No denial formed on her lips. Her boldness withered under the burden of her shame. *If I was healed, I would be worthy.*

"Is she of no concern to God?" Gil's voice grew too loud. "Does He not provide for the weak and the